<u>Hoodfellas</u>

A novel

By
Richard Jeanty

RJ Publications, LLC

Newark, New Jersey

The characters and events in this book are fictitious. Any resemblance to actual persons, living or dead, is purely coincidental.

RJ Publications
rjeantay@yahoo.com
www.rjpublications.com
Copyright © 2008 by Richard Jeanty
All Rights Reserved
ISBN **978-0978637347**

Printed in Canada

November 2008

1-2-3-4-5-6-7-8-9-10-

Acknowledgement

I would like to thank all the usual suspects who have supported me through my writing career and other endeavors. You know who you are.

To my baby girl, Rishanna, I will always love you unconditionally. Thanks for coming into my life. You have made my days brighter everyday since you came along and I'm grateful. I love you.

Special "thanks" goes out to my dad for always showing a lot of enthusiasm about my work and for continuing to sell my books to everyone that you know willing to buy it. You're my man.

I would especially like to thank Chanel Caraway and Makisha Cheeks for their special help. Without your help, I'm not sure if I could've gotten this book edited on time. Again, thank you.

Thanks go out to all the book clubs and readers who continue to inspire me to get better with each book. I would like to give a big shout- out to the street vendors, especially Abou and Pogo, and all the booksellers around the country and all over the world for keeping the world in tune with our literature. Thanks to all the book retailers and distributors who make it possible for our books to reach the people.

A special shout-out goes to all the New York book vendors and entrepreneurs. A big shout-out goes out to my nephews and nieces as well as my brothers and sisters. And last but not least, I would like to thank my fellow writers for making reading fun again for our people.

A Note To My Readers

Once again, I feel like I need to explain myself because so many of you have supported my every endeavor. As most of you already know, I don't belong in a box and I refuse to be placed in a box. And that is one of the reasons I decided to undertake this project.

Being classified as a certain type of writer belonging to a particular genre is limited to me. I'm having a lot of fun writing these different types of books and I can honestly tell you that I poured my heart into this new novel, which is my first "street novel." I never thought that I would have such a hard time with a book, but I conquered the challenge and I hope you enjoy my sweat and tears.

I have to stay one step ahead in this literary game because there are so many other talented writers out there. It is with honesty, dedication, love and hard work that I earnestly bring this book to you and I hope you enjoy it just like the rest.

As always, thanks for supporting me over the years.

Introduction

Quite a few people out there in the world get frightened at the mention of the word "gangster." This word has especially become a dirty word as it relates to African American and black people altogether.

The whole "Gangsterism" was first romanticized by Hollywood back in the 1920's when gangster movies were a booming part of the film industry. Original gangsters like Al "Scarface" Capone, George "Bugs" Moran and Dean O'Banion were revered in Hollywood because of their connection to the underworld during prohibition. Capone controlled the south side of Chicago while Moran and O'Banion established themselves on the north side. These men became gangsters because of greed, money, control and lack of opportunities, but they still had a choice.

These gangsters would take gangsterism to the next level in 1929 during the "Valentine's Day Massacre" where seven gangsters were killed execution style by Capone's gang. History has somewhat repeat itself and now we have a new era of gangsters killing more than seven people on a daily basis. However, these new gangsters should not be held responsible for creating this gangster nation.

The British were the original gangsters who came to North America, annihilated a whole race of Indians, and took over their land. This practice continued as the United States continued to expand their territories to Alaska, Puerto Rico, The Us Virgin Islands, and only the Lord knows where else they would like to conquer. Now that's some real gangster shit!

Chapter 1
The Natural Course

"Mr. Brown, we're not really here to negotiate with you. It's more like a demand, or whatever you wanna call it," said Crazy D.

"What makes you think I'm gonna do what you're telling me to do?" Mr. Brown asked. "Yo, Short Dawg, bring her out," Crazy D ordered.

Short Dawg appeared from behind Mr. Brown's storage area with a knife to Mr. Brown's wife's neck while her left hand is covered in blood. "She still has nine good fingers left, but next time we won't be cutting off fingers, oh no, we ain't interested in the same body part twice. Next time it might be one of her eyeballs hanging out the socket," Crazy D said as he signaled for Short Dawg to bring the knife to Mrs. Brown's eyes. "Tell me what you want and I'll do it, just don't hurt her," said Mr. Brown. "We've been watching you for a while now and my guesstimation is that you make about fifty to a hundred thousand dollars a month. Forty percent of that is ours and we're gonna collect it on every first of the month," he said. "How we supposed to survive? The shop doesn't even make that kind of money," Mr. Brown pleaded. "Do you need motivation to make that kind of money?" Crazy D asked as he raised his hand to Short Dawg, ordering him to start taking out one of Mrs. Brown's eyes. Before he could stick the knife in, Mr. Brown chimed in and said, "Okay, I'll do it. I'll give you forty percent of what we make." Crazy D smiled and said, "No, you'll give me forty percent of a hundred thousand dollars every month. He ordered Short Dawg to drop the knife with a swift movement of his head.

As Crazy D and Short Dawg were making their way out of the shop, Mr. Brown reached for his shotgun. However, before he could cock it back, Crazy D had his .45 Lugar in his face saying, "It's your choice, old man, you can die a hero or you can become a zero." Mr. Brown wisely placed his shotgun down, and then apologized to Crazy D. What Crazy D did to the Browns was routine since he came out of the State Pen. Crazy D walked out of jail wearing some donated clothes that were twenty years out of style and fit a little too snug around his six foot-plus frame. The difference this time was the tightness of the fit. He had gained a considerable amount of weight in muscle. The shirt was tight around his arms and his pants barely made it past his thighs. He was ridiculed as he rode the bus back to his old neighborhood. The kids were pointing at him, adults shook their heads at him and women just laughed at him. Crazy D was fed up with the treatment he received his first day out of jail. He looked like a buff homo. With no money and no skills to get a job, Crazy D had no choice but to turn back to a life of crime. After serving a twenty-year sentence for robbery and second-degree murder, the system failed him miserably, but even worse, they failed the rest of society by letting a loose canon out of jail without the proper rehabilitation.

While in jail, Cray D's mom only visited him the first few months. She soon fell victim to the crack epidemic and ultimately had to turn her back on her son at his request. There came a time when she could hardly remember that she had a son. While constantly under the influence of crack cocaine, his mother did her own stint in prison for prostitution and other petty crimes only to get out and start using again.

Crazy D went to jail at the young age of seventeen and it was there that he learned his survival tactics. Wreaking havoc on people before they got to him was what he learned when he was in prison. The attempted rape on him the first week after he arrived at the Walpole facility in Massachusetts brought his awareness to a level he never knew existed. He was lucky that one of the toughest inmates in that prison was a friend of his father's. Word had gotten out that Crazy D was being shipped to Walpole and his father's best friend made a promise to his mother to look after him. Crazy D's dad, Deon Sr., and Mean T were best friends before his dad got killed, and Mean T was sent to prison for thirty years after a botched armed robbery against a store owner.

Chapter 2
Mean T and Sticky Fingers

Mean T and Sticky Fingers aka Deon Campbell Sr. were best friends throughout their entire lives. They were more like vagrants from the time their mother decided to allow them to walk to school by themselves. In fact, the very first day that they walked to school without any supervision, they decided to make a detour to the corner store. Mean T was the lookout while Sticky Fingers robbed the store of candy, potato chips, juices and other valuables that matter to kids. It was a little distance from Evans Street to Morton Street in Dorchester, Massachusetts, but their parents trusted that they would walk directly to school everyday. The Taylor Elementary School was where most of the kids who lived on the Dorchester side of Morton Street went to school. Stealing became a fun habit for the duo and every morning they found themselves down the block at the corner store stealing more items than their pockets could afford. Mean T was the bigger of the two, but Sticky Fingers was the conniving thief. He could steal the bible from a preacher, and Mean T would knock the daylights out of a pregnant woman.

Over the years, the duo broaden their horizons from stealing candy to stealing sneakers and clothes out of a store called 42nd Street located in Mattapan Square. By then, they were in high school being promoted because of their age and not the work that they did. The two were dumb as a doorknob, but one was an expert thief and the other an enforcer. The two friends were the best young hustlers from their block. The Korean owner of the store was forced to install cameras because Sticky Fingers and Mean T kept robbing the store and there was never any proof to prosecute them. Usually, the cops didn't respond on time and by then the two had made it home safely with their stolen goods. The shop owner was growing tired of this and decided to arm himself in order to keep from getting robbed.

Mean T and Sticky Fingers wore the freshest gear to school. Everything was brand name because they stole the best of everything from the different stores downtown Boston. Their favorite stores were Filene's Jordan Marsh, Filene's Basement and of course, 42nd Street in Mattapan Square. On top of that, the two of them sold some of the stolen merchandise to some of the kids at the high school when they needed money. Their bad habit became an enterprise. The two thieves outfitted their bedrooms with stolen goods from stores all over the Boston area. They had enough merchandise to supply a whole high school of kids with clothes, shoes and other clothing items such as socks, t-shirts, underwear and long johns needed for at least a month. However, Mean T and Sticky Fingers would run into some difficulty when they decided to rob the 42nd Street store once more. The Korean owner had had enough and he felt he needed to protect his livelihood, so he bought a gun.

By this time, Mean T and Sticky Fingers were pretty known to the entire Korean family who worked as a unit in the store. While Sticky Fingers walked around and stuffed his bag with stolen items, so he could dash out of the store using the same tactics they had used in the past with Mean T knocking out the father who stood guard at the entrance, the father looked on. However, on this day, they would meet their fate. As Sticky Fingers rushed towards the exit, all he felt was a hot bullet piercing through his heart. Mean T didn't even have time to react as the small Korean man raised his gun and stuck it in Mean T's mouth. Pandemonium rang out in the store as everyone tried to make it to the exit. Meanwhile, Sticky Finger's lifeless body lay on the ground with his hands clutched around a duffle bag filled with stolen items. The cops arrived in no time. Someone's life had to be taken in order for the cops to respond in a timely manner.

Mr. Chang, as the community later found out the store owner's name, had to defend himself against the whole community. No one came to his defense when he was being robbed blindly, but everyone was angry because another young black life had been taken. Sticky Finger's mom came out shedding tears as if she didn't know what her son was doing in the street. A search of the victim's home revealed about fifty thousand dollars worth of stolen items from different stores, including Mr. Chang's 42nd Street. Sticky Finger's mom had to have known that her son was hawking stolen merchandise because the officers could barely take a step into his room without stepping over stolen clothes while serving the search warrant. The whole place was cluttered with clothes scattered all over the room.

To top off an already insane situation, the cops found a loaded gun on Mean T after searching him at the scene. Mean T aka Tony Gonsalves, an American born Cape Verde heritage young man was handcuffed and taken to jail where he faced aggravated robbery, illegal possession of a handgun, first degree armed robbery and a list of other charges concocted by the district attorney to ensure his proper place away from society for the next thirty years. It didn't help that Tony and Deon weren't in good standing at school. No teachers, counselor or principal would vouch for them as good people. The media smeared their names even further and there was no way that Tony was going to walk even though his friend was killed.

A few months after Deon's murder, the media revealed that he had left behind a pregnant woman with an unborn child. That child would be named Deon after his father. Mean T would receive a thirty-year sentence, the maximum allowed under Massachusetts law. He was transferred from the correctional facility in Concord to the facility in Walpole after his sentence. As a young man, Mean T didn't really understand the extent of his sentence, so he chose to act in a machismo way and accepted his fate. On the van ride from Concord to Walpole, while shackled to other hardcore criminals, reality started to set in for Mean T and he understood clearly that his life had taken a drastic turn for the worst and he had better start thinking about his survival tactics. Mean T rose to prominence very quickly at the prison as he engaged some of the tougher inmates in fights and defeated quite a few of them while earning their respect.

Mean T was tested very day he was headed to Walpole to start his sentence. One repeated offender wanted to impress all the impressionable first timers in the van, and he made the unthinkable mistake of picking on Meant T. "You're gonna be my bitch when we touch down," he said to Mean T with a tempted grin. The whole van was laughing except Meant T. He was sitting in the row in front of Mean T and had to turn his neck around to talk to him. Before he could turn around to say something else, Mean T threw his handcuffed hands around his neck and choked him until he passed out. Words had gotten around about the incident and Mean T was given his props for almost killing a man who was known as Nutty Harold in prison. Nutty Harold was released on a technicality and he unfortunately had a confrontation with Mean T on his way back to prison after killing a man six months out of prison.

It was almost eighteen years later, a few months short of his eighteenth birthday, when Crazy D aka Deon Campbell Jr. would walk into the prison in Walpole to meet the guardian angel known to him as Abdul Mustafa Muhammad. Mean T had converted to Islam while serving his sentence. He had gotten into many fights after arriving at the prison, including one that involved sending a prison guard to the emergency room, which earned him an additional ten years to his sentence. Mean T was casually walking to his cell after code red was called. This one particular guard, who hated him for garnering the respect of his fellow inmates, felt Mean T was not walking fast enough. He use his stick to rush Mean T back to his cell thinking that the other two guards behind him provided a safe haven from an asswhip. Mean T was much too quick and strong for the guard as he found his neck wrapped inside Mean T's massive biceps. The two guards stood back as Mean T threatened to choke the life out of the guard who unjustly pushed and hit him with the stick. The white guard started turning pink and his eyes bulging out of their sockets as he fainted from the chokehold feeling that life itself was about to end. The other two guards could only watch in horror before stepping in to provide some relief for the guard using their night stick. He became a lifer. Abdul, formerly known as Tony Gonsalves also formerly known as Mean T on the streets, was a highly respected man in prison. As a lifer, he had earned the reputation of a tough, intelligent and manipulating leader. He protected those close to him and destroyed those who went against him.

Chapter 3
Serena Bender

Serena was an impressionable young girl when she met the bad boy known as Sticky Fingers. He smote her right away because of his caring ways. She did not call him by his street name, Sticky Fingers, because she thought it was demeaning, but Deon wore the name with pride. Deon's fervor for life was what Serena admired most about him. He was spontaneous and lived carelessly, completely opposite of how she was raised. Sticky Fingers' approach was also very different from the other young men who tried to talk to Serena. Standing at 5ft 5inches tall with perky C size cups, a small waist and ass for generations, Serena stood out from the rest of the girls. Her caramel complexion and blemish free skin gave her a pristine glow. Sticky Fingers met her at the bus stop everyday with her favorite candy, M&M's, in his hands. She especially liked the ones with peanuts, and every morning Sticky Fingers would steal four packs from the convenience store and handed them to Serena. He claimed that he bought them, but she knew very well why his name was Sticky Fingers. The bad boy allure appealed to her and she didn't care whether or not he stole the candy. It just melted in her mouth every morning and Sticky Fingers couldn't wait for her to take his tongue in her mouth.

At sixteen years old, Serena only had one prior sexual experience with a boy who took her virginity, so Sticky Fingers would be her second. Serena never let the cat out the bag that she was sexually active. She acted as if Sticky Fingers was her first. Actually, in her mind, she felt Sticky Fingers was her first because the first guy was a bit rough and she didn't enjoy the experience at all. "Don't tell me that I done pulled a virgin?" Sticky

Fingers said excitedly in between kisses with Serena during their first physical encounter. The passion between them started on the back of the bus where they shared a seat everyday on the way to and from school, whenever Sticky felt like being in school, that is. Everybody knew they were a couple. Sticky was overly protective of Serena and would threaten any guy who even looked at her funny. He wasn't the most attractive guy, but his bad boy flair made him attractive to some of the women at the high school.

After getting off the school bus everyday, Serena and Sticky Fingers would walk hand in hand straight to his house. His mother wasn't home as usual and he felt it was the best opportunity for him to rock Serena's world. One day while Serena waited in the living room for Sticky, she looked through his old photo album to see even more atrocious-looking pictures of him as a little boy. He had improved ten fold in the looks department, and that was not much. Sticky Fingers came back to the living room carrying a Louis Vuitton bag filled with brand name clothes and a floral baby-doll with lace trim and adjustable straps that he had stolen earlier in the week from Jordan Marsh. Sticky Fingers had charms, a lot of stolen goods, and he knew the only way to get Serena's panties wet was to break out with the gift bag. Like a typical hood chick, Serena was impressed with all the brand name items in the bag, including a pair of high end Gucci boots that Sticky Fingers stole from the Gucci store on Newbury Street. Some people are still amazed as to how he was even able to steal from any store on Newbury Street. Usually, Negroes like him were carefully watched after entering any store on that street. It's a street that is frequented by rich white folks with enough money to wipe out poverty in all of the ghettos of Boston.

After Serena pulled the boots out of the bag, a light bulb went off in Sticky Fingers' head and he suddenly had a smirk on his face. "Damn, those boots are fly. Everybody's gonna be sweating me when they see me in these boots with my Jordache Jeans," she said. "Yeah, baby, you're gonna look hot, but I want you to look even hotter for me now. I want you to put on that babydoll and those boots while you stroll to my room. Serena had a choice to make, either she could turn down about two thousand dollars worth of fly shit, or she could play her little role and give the coochie to Sticky Fingers and keep all the fly shit that her pussy was getting wet over. She went with the latter, confirming that she was leaving his house sexed up with a Louis Vuitton bag and enough shit to have even her girlfriends want to give some pussy to Sticky Fingers. Hoodrats sleep with men for material items, and Serena was definitely a Hoodrat in training.

Living in the Morton Street project, she had no other choice. All her friends were Hoodrats, and the guys in her neighborhood were thugs or drug dealers, what the hell was she going to do?

A quick trip to the bathroom to change from her tight jeans to her fly boots and baby doll was enough to set Sticky Fingers' blood boiling with anticipation. At eighteen years old, his ten-inch dick was overflowing with blood and he couldn't wait to stick it all in Serena's pussy. Sticky Fingers had been planning this day for a while. It started with the M&M's then he graduated to giving Serena her lunch money everyday and then moved on to getting her hair done regularly. It was his biggest spending spree yet and he wanted to be compensated with some pussy. Sticky Fingers slipped out of his clothes while Serena was in the bathroom. He was sitting on the couch butt-naked while still wearing his shell toe Adidas and a rope chain around his neck, typical gangster shit. Serena stepped out of the bathroom to find a hard ten-inch dick ready to tear her pussy in half. Sticky Fingers was salivating all over her ass.

The shocked look on Serena's face after glancing at Sticky Fingers' huge dick confirmed that fear existed in her mind. Sticky Fingers wanted to play down that fear. These gift items weren't gonna come as easy as she thought. As he took a puff from a joint he had been smoking while she was in the bathroom, he felt relaxed. "Would you like to take a puff?" he offered her. Like a typical hoodrat, she wasn't about to turn down the chance to get high off somebody else's shit. "Sure," she said. After smoking the joint down to a roach, it was time for Sticky Finger to get into that wet hole that his dick had been standing up for all this time. He pulled Serena towards him and planted a rough kiss on her lips like he was acting out a scene out of a bad porno flick. Serena was not pleased but she kept her mouth shut because the valuables in that Louis Vuitton bag would be all worth it. He tugged on her lips with his and didn't even pay attention to the painful signs on Serena's face. He then quickly made his way down to her breasts and started sucking on them like a hungry kid from Somalia. He was about to suck her titties dry, painfully, until she asked, "Do you have a condom?" "I'm sure I can find one in my room," he responded. While her breast was relinquished from his mouth, she lay across the couch flat on her back, suggesting that she wanted to get the shit over and done with. "Why you laying on yo back already?" he asked. "Aren't you about to do it?" she asked. "Yeah, but not before I get a blowjob from you," he said. "I ain't sucking yo dick. I don't suck dick. We can fuck, but I ain't sucking yo dick," she said. "Why it gotta be like that?" he asked. "Are you gonna eat my pussy?

I'll suck your dick if you eat my pussy. I ain't gonna have you tell everybody I sucked your dick and you ain't eat my pussy," she said. "Hell naw! I ain't eating yo pussy. We just gonna have to fuck then," he said. All Sticky Fingers really wanted was to bust a nut in Serena's big ass, anyway.

Sticky Fingers ran to his room to look for a condom, but he couldn't find any. That bastard knew damn well that he had never used a condom before and there was no condom in his room. "I can't find my condoms," he said after emerging from his room. "I guess we ain't fucking. I ain't trying to be pregnant by you," she said. Sticky Fingers was determined to taste that pussy and there was no way Serena was walking out of the house without giving him some. He had to pull all the stops. He went back to his room and came back with a two-carat tennis bracelet that he had stolen from Filene's. "I was gonna give you this for your birthday, but you can have it now. I just wanna show you how much I like you," he said. Her eyes lit up and a smile flashed across her face as the diamonds sparkled in her pupils. Sticky Fingers was now sitting on the couch and one of his fingers was doing major damage to Serena's pussy. "Mmm, ooh, ah," she faked her moans. She knew Sticky Fingers was going to be rough with her from the movement of his fingers inside her pussy. The brother acted like he was digging for gold. Giving up the pussy was a must as the two-carat tennis bracelet was shining around her wrist and taking it off was not an option. She braced herself as he shoved his ten-inch, rock hard dick inside her. "I promise I will pull out before I come," he said. She lay there completely in pain waiting for the signal when he was about to come so she could push him off her. However, the instant he inserted his dick was the same instant his semen spurt out without as much as a stroke. As his body shivered less than a second into her, she wondered if it was his own style of a pelvic movement not knowing that he had prematurely ejaculated.

He lay on top of her, humping her with his dick still hard because of adolescence, and finally he was able to pick up the speed of his strokes as he started forcefully fucking her to get a second nut. She grimaced as he pounded her with brute force. "I wanna do it doggy-style," he said. She turned over on her stomach, giving him complete control. It was one painful smack after another against her buttocks before he started screaming five minutes, "I'm coming!" as if he had accomplished something. She quickly pulled away from him as he splattered semen all over her ass.

Serena found herself pregnant six weeks later as Deon completely denied his possible involvement in contributing to the pregnancy. He told her that there was no way that she could be pregnant by him because he had pulled out of her before he came. That lying bastard knew that his second lasting ass more than came inside Serena, but he didn't want to take on the responsibility of a child, at first. Faced with single parenthood and the possibility of being a high school dropout, Serena's best option was an abortion. However, avoiding a repeated cycle was easier said than done. Serena grew up in the projects with a teenage mother who collected welfare since she was born and didn't have to worry about getting up everyday to go to work because the government and the hustlers she was fucking kept her rent paid and food on the table. Serena had seen the hustle and it was her turn to establish her own independence and hustle. Her mother was never short on weed and fashion. The many hustlers she offered pussy to in exchange for what she needed was enough to keep her living the ghetto fabulous lifestyle. Stores like JC Penney and Marshall's were a luxury for her and she would brag to her daughter every time one of her men would take her shopping there. "These men will do anything for that good pussy. You have to make sure you don't give your pussy away for free," she would tell her daughter. And Serena was definitely paying attention and taking notes from her mother.

Before welfare reform, pregnant women could receive free housing at the cost of decent tax payers and Serena wanted to take advantage of that. She didn't hear from Deon for about six weeks after she told him about her pregnancy, but he soon started coming back and was buying items for the baby. He was looking forward to having a child and he stole everything that he could that a baby would need, including a crib. She stopped going to school and was looking forward to having her own apartment in the projects down the street from her mother. That ultimately meant that she would have more freedom to do whatever the hell she wanted. Since Deon didn't like school, he started spending more time with her and fucking her as much as he could during the day whenever her mother was not around. They started growing closer to each other and Deon had even made a promise to marry Serena before the baby was born.

However, that marriage would never take place and Deon would never get a chance to see his child. It was while she was watching the six-o'clock news that Serena heard of Deon's death. Earlier in the day, he told her he was going downtown and that he would come back later to see her. Those were the last words he said to her before he left her house. Serena was about seven months pregnant and her child would never have a father. She couldn't change his destiny even though she finally offered to give him a blowjob if he stayed home with her that morning. Whatever he had planned was far more important that day than the blowjob that he had been bugging her about. "I'll take that blowjob later," he jokingly said to her before walking out the apartment. "I ain't sucking your dick later. You only getting this offer once, Deon," she screamed to him as he hurried down the hall.

After giving birth to a healthy baby boy at Boston City Hospital, Serena decided to honor Deon by naming her son after him. Deon Campbell Jr. was welcomed into the world by his mother and grandmother. Deon had stolen enough goods for his baby before he died, so Serena didn't have to worry about a thing for the first few months. Soon, the baby formula started running out and her mother was getting frustrated with her because there was an extra mouth to feed. As soon as the baby started crying, Serena's mother took her down to the welfare office to apply for assistance. After a couple of months, she was provided with a two-bedroom apartment and food stamps to help care for her baby.

As soon as Serena got her own apartment, things started getting out of hand. Life on welfare was tough and Serena wanted more. The food stamps and small allowance she was given every two weeks barely kept her head above water. She needed to something before she drowned. The only other alternative to her situation was for Serena to get a job. With no education or work experience, Serena was faced with the possibility of only earning a minimum wage salary at the local McDonald's or Burger King. The amount of money she would earn working full-time at McDonald's would barely surpass her welfare benefits and she would be cut off from welfare. Not willing to give up free assistance, Serena's decision wasn't difficult at all; she decided to continue to collect her welfare check while hustling on the side.

Chapter 4
Hustling

Serena met Tremaine at a birthday party in the projects. He was a lean, tall, skinny kid and a fast-talker who believed in keeping himself looking super def all the time with the freshest gear that his money could buy. When Serena met him, he was wearing a pair of blue Guess Jeans, orange Polo shirt, blue and orange Patrick Ewing Adidas and a blue Kangol hat to match his outfit. Everybody took notice of the skinny kid known affectionately to everyone as Tre. As a matter of fact, Tre had contributed to the party. He provided the Heineken that all the underage drinkers were drinking. The birthday girl was a big booty chick that Tremaine had been fucking for a while, and he had no choice but to reciprocate with the beers. That night, however, Tre saw new pussy and a new opportunity. A man with his mind always on his money, Tre had heard about Serena being a high maintenance project chick. Serena had also heard about Tre's reputation as a weed dealer who was making enough cash to provide the lifestyle she yearned for.

Guys like Tre couldn't have just one woman. He had women on every corner of that project. It didn't hurt that the ladies used to brag about his ten-inch dick like it was a diamond. Standing six-feet tall at about one hundred and forty pounds, Tre was almost scrawny. However, for some reason, women believe that scrawny men have big dicks and Tre definitely reinforced that myth. The song "Fly Girl" was blaring through the speakers as Tre made his way towards Serena. Nobody could stand still to that song back then. Serena was demonstrating her skills as she stood there grinding and humping the air to Tre's satisfaction. He didn't even ask if he could dance with her, he just went behind her and started grinding. She welcomed his crotch as support as she leaned back and started grinding on his dick. With the lights barely bright enough in the room to see anything, all the men lined the wall with a woman standing in front of them while smacking, rubbing and tapping their asses like it was a swingers' party.

Back then, everyone partied with the lights low or completely off because the horny teens wanted to get their feel on without the embarrassment of everybody knowing what they were doing. Oh, how things have changed. Tre soon found his dick rising against Serena's ass and she pushed back even harder on it to confirm to Tre that his advances were welcomed. It was also customary for the DJ to play a slow jam back then to allow everybody to get their grind on. "Let's Get it On" by Marvin Gaye was the song of the hour and

Serena turned around and placed her arms around Tre's shoulder while he reached down to palm her ass with his hands as they grinded on each other.

Meanwhile, the birthday girl was walking all around the room looking for Tre because she knew she was his honorary "fuck" for the night. Unfortunately, Tre was like any other man, there was nothing like new pussy, which was the motto that he lived by as a drug dealer. Tre was the typical drug dealer who juggled many different women at once. Tre would shield himself from the birthday girl or moved around whenever she was getting close to finding him in the dark. He was careful and only shoved his tongue down Serena's throat when the coast was clear. The fun thing about those parties back then was the "anything goes" attitude. People came to have fun and party without worrying about gunfire or a big fight over nothing. Back then people partied 'til dawn and Serena took advantage of the fact that her mother had agreed to watch little Deon for her that night. By the time she left the party, she knew that Tre would soon be getting some pussy from her, and Tre knew that the pussy was his to take.

As much as Tre would've liked to believe that he had Serena in the palm of his hands, she was more concerned about the money he was making through hustling. These project chicks didn't give the booty up without any type of financial assistance. To boost their claim, the song "No Romance without Finance" was a big hit at the time. There was nothing going on but the rent, and Tre was about to pay up for the booty. Serena decided she would become a hustler on the night she met Tre. She understood the game and it was a matter of just learning how to play it. Numbers were exchanged and she knew full and well that Tre was going to be banging the birthday girl while he had his mind on her.

After giving birth to little Deon, Serena's thighs expanded and her ass busted out like she had implants way before J-Lo brought booty implants en vogue, baby girl was looking good. Her plans were to use what her mama gave her to get what she wanted. Tre soon fell victim to her thighs and before he knew it, she was collecting money from him on a regular basis. Serena had become somewhat of a high priced ho, sexing only ballers, drug dealers and men with enough money to offer her the finer things in life.

She wasn't fazed by good or bad dick. She stroked a few egos when she had to and she enjoyed good sex when she needed to. It was never personal; it was always about her money. Without realizing it, her hustle started with Sticky Fingers and slowly progressed to the state where she was now sexing as many as five men a week to feed her cravings for the finer things in life. Serena's hustle, although started on a small scale, was now netting her about a couple thousand dollars a week. Her partners came in all shapes, sizes, colors and background. Tre may have positioned himself as one of her regulars because of his sexual prowess, but his money wasn't long enough to see her as often as he wanted. She fucked him about twice a week, once for money and the other for pleasure. Tre always delivered and Serena loved his long strokes. She also lied when he wanted to see more of her. She used her son as an excuse not to see him as often as he would like.

Serena had one man paying for little Deon's daycare every week plus fringe benefits. This guy named Maurice who worked as a foreman for a construction company had more than enough money to help support Serena and her son, but he was married with five children of his own. Serena became the excuse that he used when he needed to work overtime. He worked overtime all right, on her pussy. Maurice would come over and enjoy Serena's tight pussy every Monday and Thursday during his lunch hour. He was working on a construction project not too far from Serena's apartment. They met while Serena was walking to the corner store to get some milk for her son. Not one to ever be caught off guard, Serena never left her house looking homely. She wore one of her favorite pair of tight jeans that day with a shirt that barely covered her chest. She had no stretch mark after giving birth. It was the typical whistling from the construction workers as she walked past the site. Maurice was away from the herd when all the commotion was going on. He noticed that she was headed to the store, so he beat her there. "Hey, how ya doing?" he said to her. "I'm fine," she answered casually. "My name is Maurice, what's yours?" he asked. "My name is Serena, can I help you with something?" she said with an inviting attitude. "I'm just trying to get to know a fine lady, that's all," Maurice said. As Serena placed the gallon of milk and a box of Gerber on the counter, Maurice asked, "Do you have a baby?" Serena answered, "Yes." "Well, I'm sure your baby probably needs some diapers too. Why don't you grab some and I'll take care of it. Not one to turn down a free offer, Serena went to the back and grabbed the biggest box of diapers she could find.

Maurice gladly paid for Serena's purchase. Before he left the store, he wrote his number on a piece of paper and handed it to her. As Serena made her way back home, she was giddy. She had just met another sucker who saved her a few dollars, but she knew that Maurice was worth more than that. His round build and chubby face gave him the aura of a sugar bear, a sugar daddy that is. Within weeks, Maurice and Serena were going out to some of the nicest restaurants to eat. He would always offer to pay for a babysitter to take her out. Half of the fifty bucks he gave her for a sitter usually went to her mother for watching her son. Serena milked the situation for as long as she could before finally giving up the pussy to Maurice. He wasn't as well endowed as Tre, but he was a lot more skilled. He ate her pussy like his favorite chicken and she came more with Maurice than any man. His dick game wasn't as tight as his tongue game. He came up a little short in the energy and length department. He'd fuck her well but his dick wasn't satisfying enough and stamina was weak. He would always cum before she got hers and she hated that. However, Maurice's generosity gave him an open door policy to Serena's pussy.

There were other hustles, but Serena decided that hustling men would be her best asset. Armed with a beautiful face, body and street smarts, Serena over time started to look to men with the financial status of "ballers." There was nothing else she figured she could do and Serena wanted to make sure her bills got paid and then some. She slowly eased Tre out of her life as he had become a petty dealer to her. It was no longer about the cheap hollow gold and knock-off brands of clothing that he could buy her; she wanted real money. Even Maurice found himself questioning where he went wrong when Serena told him that she would no longer be his concubine. Offers of an extra hundred dollars a week made no difference as Serena had already found a baller by the name of Wally who was giving her a thousand times the amount of money she received from both Tre and Maurice.

Wally was the real McCoy. A big time hustler who was known for his generosity with the ladies, he blessed Serena with a fur coat the first time after they went out. The most surprising thing and what gave him a permanent key to Serena's pussy was the fact that he stuffed an envelope with twenty thousand dollars in cash in the coat's pocket. It was more money than Serena had seen her entire life. In other words, the pussy went to the highest bidder and Wally bought it straight out that night.

Though Wally was balling out of control, making close to a quarter of a million dollars a week selling drugs up and down the east coast, his premature ejaculation was a huge problem for Serena. His dick would greet Serena's pussy hair and within seconds, he'd be releasing ounces of protein all over her stomach. There was one particular incident when Serena reached for his dick to thank him for yet another generous gesture when he had a new living-room set delivered to her house. Her tongue went around the shaft of his dick only once before he released his thick semen down her throat. Serena knew that sexual pleasure for herself would never come from Wally. He had very little time and the only control that he had had to be on the street because he sure as hell didn't have any dick control. This went on for the better part of six months before Serena grew frustrated with Wally always coming without taking into consideration her own needs. Eating Serena's pussy was out of the question because Wally only ate one pussy his whole life and that was his wife's. Whether he was even good at that, is another story.

Chapter 5

In Search of Pleasure

Even though Serena had kicked Maurice out of her life, it seemed like he was lurking around. Naturally, when Serena felt the need to get her sexual needs satisfied, she called the only man who ate her pussy well enough to satisfy her. Maurice was more than amused when he received a call from Serena requesting a rendezvous for sex. Serena was smart enough to know that she couldn't shit where she slept. So she asked Maurice to get a hotel room for their sexual romp. Since Wally paid in full for her pussy, he also had full access to her place; he could come and go as he pleased because he had his own keys. It was a good thing that there were no cell-phones back then because Serena would not have been able to get away to the hotel to let Maurice fuck her.

Maurice was elated as he made the reservation for the room at the Suisse Chalet on Morrissey Boulevard in Dorchester. With his dick rock hard in his pants, he looked forward to meeting with Serena at six o'clock that evening. She had made it clear to Maurice that it was going to be a sex thing and nothing more, but Maurice was hoping to for something more. He had missed Serena and wanted her back. He was determined to tear up Serena's pussy that evening to make her come back to him. He stopped at the Chinese store in Chinatown to get a small bottle of Stud spray to numb his dick to keep him from coming. It was known back then that these guys in Boston used the Stud spray regularly when they wanted to impress a woman. The only side effect to the spray, was that they couldn't receive a blowjob. It wasn't like

Serena enjoyed sucking Maurice's dick anyway, and he knew this.

As planned, Serena showed up right on time. Maurice was already in the room attempting to create a miracle to try to get rid of a gut that he had obtained over a lifetime by doing a few sit-ups. His body was glistening after he stepped out of the shower wearing a pair of silk boxers with his protruded gut being slightly sucked in as he answered the door to her knock. A bottle of champagne was on ice on the table and a fresh dozen of roses sat in a vase on the nightstand next to the bed with a card. "Look at you, trying to get all romantic and shit. I just came to get my shit off and be out," Serena said as she stepped through the door. "Now, I can't do nothing nice for you anymore," Maurice retorted. "I already told you that I can't be getting all involved with you the way I used to before. I got a good thing and I want to keep it. I'm just here to get my pussy eaten and some dick from you," she said. "Damn, you're making me feel like a piece of meat. Can I at least get a hug?" he asked. She walked over and gave him a hug, and while hugging him she reached down his crotch to grab his already hardened dick. Serena was trying as hard as she could to take the romance out of the situation. There was a possibility that she may never give the booty up to Maurice ever again.

"Can you at least read the card that I got you?" he told her. "Maurice, you know I can't be taking no card and these flowers with me. Why we can't just fuck with no strings attached?" she said to him. Maurice's blood was starting to boil, but his temperature quickly went down upon the sight of Serena's bouncing titties and nice, round and firm ass. Serena grabbed a glass filled with champagne and guzzled it down like she was trying to get her mind ready for what she was about to do. She lay across the bed with her legs spread wide open and her pinkness staring Maurice right in the face and said, "I want you to eat me." Maurice had never seen that forceful side of Serena. She appeared to be more in control than he was and he lost equilibrium. He quickly got on bended knees and went to work like he was ordered. Maurice's tongue-strokes were voracious as he licked the erected clit of Serena while sticking his index finger inside her. "That's what I'm talking about," she moaned as Maurice gave her something that she had been missing for the last six months or so since she met Wally." With his ego completely stroked and his best performance on the horizon, Maurice leaped straight into her pussy with his tongue as he massaged her clit with his fingers. Her sweet nectar was nostalgia to his nose as he sucked lightly on her succulent pussy lips. "Don't be stretching my pussy lips too much 'cause I don't want to get in trouble when I get home," she told him. Maurice was skillful when it came to eating pussy and he knew that he could only get rid of Wally by leaving the evidence of over-stretched pussy lips for Wally to see when she got home. So he continued to massage her clit as he lightly suck her pussy lips, forcing them to swell up and extend, but Serena couldn't stop him because the simultaneous movement of his index finger inside her pussy, his thumb on her clit and his mouth sucking on her pussy lips was too much pleasure for her to stop him.

"If it's one thing that you do well, it's eating my pussy," she said as Maurice forced a nut out of her with the circular motion of his finger on her clit. She held on to his head and started winding all over his face as she came. Maurice was smiling inside because he thought his sexual prowess would have her crawling back to him. He forgot the one important thing; cunnilingus wasn't the only thing she wanted, she also wanted penetration and Maurice's penetration game was sub par.

After Serena mounted him for what she hoped would be a pussy-filled pleasure ride, she was sadly disappointed as Maurice fell short of her expectations. Sure, he was rock hard and ready to put in work, but his dick lacked length and width and the only person who ever filled that void was Tre. Serena was now realizing that money wasn't enough to keep her happy. She was also becoming a sexual being and she wanted to be satisfied sexually as well. She soon found herself running between Tre and Maurice for sexual satisfaction while Wally satisfied her financial needs. She received great penetration from Tre while Maurice remained her oral stimuli. Wally was also becoming repulsive to her as he made no effort to improve his bedroom skills. She felt like a whore who had to have sex with him because of the guilty pleasures he provided for her.

Serena was no longer walking because Wally had blessed her with a brand new 3 series BMW. She was also becoming familiar with the Copley mall as well as Newbury Street, a trendy spot for shopping in Boston. While she may have had the money to shop at these exclusive shops, she lacked the class necessary to fit into that crowd. Everything she bought was gaudy. If the Christian Dior logo couldn't be read a mile away by adoring fans, there was no reason for her to buy it. She became a walking billboard for high fashion. Jordache was spread across her ass, while Gucci and Izod took over her chest as she strutted around Boston like she was some kind of ghetto princess.

Between short trips to Tre and Maurice's house Wally became suspicious of Serena because she started to become distant. She also made the mistake of calling Maurice from her home phone once. While she went to the bathroom to freshen up for Wally as it was a customary demand of his that she always washed her pussy before he touched her, Wally pressed redial on her phone and Maurice answered with, "Hi baby." That was all that needed to be said. Wally knew that she was cheating on him. Serena also didn't think that Wally was going to make an unexpected stop at her house while she was on the phone with Maurice. She had to hurriedly whisper to Maurice, "I'll call you back in 10 minutes." Maurice, with an expected grin thought Serena was calling him back when he picked up his phone, talking about "Hi baby." Caller ID has made the game so easy, some folks just don't understand. He had no idea who was calling and assumed the best.

While Serena thought she was coming out the bathroom wearing a brand new black teddy to surprise Wally, she was sadly disappointed when her left eye met the fury of his fist. Nothing was said as a barrage of smacks and punches with thunderous strength hit her face and body. She didn't even have time to scream as Wally knocked her unconscious and started saying to her, "No bitch is gonna disrespect me. I pay for this pussy. This is my pussy, ho. I'mma teach you not to fuck with a player. I buy you jewelry, cars, furniture and put money in your pocket and you think you can go out and fuck some other cat? Fuck you bitch." Those were the last words he said to her before stomping his right foot against her head crushing it against the floor.

Chapter 6

Consequences

Serena hadn't been the same since the beating she received from Wally. Her deranged face no longer appealed to Maurice or Tre and she was too scared to report the incident to the police, because she knew Wally could get rid of her in a New York minute. She also suffered from tremendous head trauma and seemed to have lost her hearing since that day. Serena's relationship with Wally lasted for about seven years before she was found out. During the relationship, Wally did everything he possibly could with his drug money to make sure Serena and Deon Jr. were fine. Deon Jr. wore the finest kids' clothes that money could buy and played with the best toys. By the time he entered grade school, he had become a spoiled little brat who wanted everything, and his mother made sure he had everything because Wally's money was paying for it. Serena really had a good thing going until she allowed her sexual urges to cloud her judgment.

By the time Wally decided to walk out of her life after leaving her almost lifeless on the living room floor, Serena's life had no direction. First, she became a booster in order to try to maintain the lifestyle that she had, but she wasn't the best at it. She got caught stealing so many times that a court judge was willing to send her away for five years. She soon realized that she could lose custody of her son, so she decided to try something else. Serena started slinging rocks for Tre who was by then on his way up the street-pharmaceutical latter. He was no longer interested in Serena's pussy, but he knew that she could make him some money on the block. Serena also started hanging with a group of people who did nothing but smoke weed and drink malt liquor. Her house was usually filled with people on the weekends and most of the time she provided the weed and the booze from the money she made selling drugs.

Once, Serena and her friends got so high and so wasted that someone came in and robbed them. They also found a $5000.00 stash that she was holding for Tre. When Serena woke up the next morning, she didn't know who had robbed her and she got pissed with all her drinking buddies and asked them all to get the fuck outta her house. Still in a drunken stupor, she ran around the house looking for the $5000.00 dollars she had hidden in a shoebox, but even worse, they also took the 9oz of crack cocaine she had in a bag in her closet. She was flat broke and owed Tre five grand along with the drugs.

Later that evening Tre showed up to collect his money, but the only thing that Serena could offer him was a blowjob, for which he showed no interest. By then, Tre was fucking the finest hoodrats and chickenheads that Boston had to offer. His money was bigger than before and he now was sporting a five series BMW with chrome wheels and all the other flashy accessories associated with status in the game. He could've put a sign on his back that said "I'm a drug dealer. Lock me up." With his mind on his money and money on his mind, Tre wasn't gonna let Serena get away with his money. He may not have been a pimp but Serena was gonna suck enough dicks until he got his money. Dudes started paying up to get their dick sucked by Serena and she had to do it to get even with Tre. He forced her into prostitution.

Meanwhile, Deon Jr. encountered all kinds of hustlers talking all types of shit in his ear as he grew up in the projects at his mom's house. His mom never once thought about the affect and consequences of her actions. Deon once saw his mom on her knees sucking this neighborhood kid's dick and he was so disgusted, he stayed under the bed for the whole day. The kid was a 17-year-old street corner hustler for Tre. By the time Serena was able to pay Tre back all his money, her services as a corner pusher were no longer needed as she'd started smoking rocks herself. The same kids whose dicks she used to suck started paying her with rocks instead of money for blowjobs. Life as Serena knew it started changing for her and everything went downhill.

Hadn't it been for Serena's grandmother making sure that Deon was okay, the state would've gotten custody of him and he would have ended up in foster care. Perhaps that would've been the best thing for him. His grandmother never wanted the full responsibility of raising him because she was still in her forties and getting her groove on with some of the old hustlers from the hood. She tried as much as she could to help her daughter, but Serena was a lost case.

Deon had to learn to care for himself by the time he was nine years old. Food was always scarce in the house because Serena wasted her food stamps on crack. When Deon Jr. started stealing food from the local grocery store, it was because he really needed to. Waking up everyday and going to school on an empty stomach not only affected his adjustment at school, but it also altered his personality. Deon Jr. was never a normal child because he had to learn to care for himself at a young age. Since he was left on his own, stealing was the only thing that he could do to eat. His grandmother claimed she cared, but she didn't care enough to take him in. She would offer help and look after him only when one of her beau's wasn't willing to come by and get a quick nut from her.

By the time Deon Jr. became an adolescent, jail was inevitable. He had already become a product of his environment. Having to steal to eat, developed into a full-blown habit of robbing and stealing without remorse. Deon's fate was sealed when his mother decided to take that crack pipe to her mouth.

Over the years, Serena had a hard time remembering that she even had a son. When Deon Jr. went to prison, it was the grandmother who kept reminding her that she had to go to the prison to see Deon Jr. every now and then. Deon Jr. had a hard time dealing with his mother's condition while he was in prison, so he decided to ask her to stop coming to the prison to see him. Her state of mind seemed to have been somewhere else every time he saw her and it was hard for him to swallow. Deon had been denied the opportunity to be raised by his mother because of drugs and he knew he wanted to get back at all those people who caused pain and grief to his family one day.

Once Serena found solace in the crack pipe, her life had been deteriorating from that point. She did too many stints in jail while Crazy D was locked up. Her longest bid was a three-year bid for armed robbery. She robbed a white woman of her purse at knifepoint and it only took the cops twenty minutes to find her with the woman's wallet still in her possession. After being released from jail, Serena returned to the life that she knew best, robbery, drugs, and prostitution. Serena had fallen victim to her own vices. She never even had a chance. Serena ended up having to serve a twenty-year sentence.

Chapter 7
Crazy D

The name Crazy D didn't appear on Deon's birth certificate, he earned it on the street. From the age of twelve, he started breaking into people's houses stealing televisions, VCR's and anything else valuable he could get his hands on. The guy was a natural kleptomaniac. He even tried to steal his teacher's watch right off her hand once. The name Crazy D came about in the early 90's. Deon had broken in so many homes; people in the neighborhood had to put steel bars on their windows and alarms in their homes. Everybody thought he was crazy, but he became certifiably crazy to everyone the day that he decided to steal a police car. Someone had gotten shot down the block on Evans Street and as police officers tried to close off the area to start their investigation, Crazy D jumped into one of the police cruisers and took off down the street as his mother begged helplessly for him to stop. "Deon, stop!" his mother screamed, but Deon was all about the thrill. He wasn't just missing a screw, he was completely screwed up.

The tires screeched as he peeled out from the scene burning rubber like he was shooting a stunt for a dangerous scene of an action movie. The whole neighborhood looked in disbelief as he took off in the cruiser. The incident was soon called in by the cops and a chase ensued. Deon's crazy ass came back around the block to display his defiance for the law to his neighbors. One of the cops tried to release a warning shot into the front tire as Deon hit the gas pedal heading towards him. Before he could aim a second time, he was about a mili-second from getting hit, so he jumped out the way as Deon went on a rampage hitting every parked car on that street. He continued down the street until he lost control of the car and ended up crashing against a big tree that stood at the end of the street. Police surrounded him with guns drawn and Deon aka Crazy D had seen his last day as a free man.

A slew of charges, including, aggravated assault with a dangerous weapon: a police car, and attempted murder for trying to run down a police officer. Many other charges were brought up against him in court by the district attorney and Deon Campbell Jr. found himself facing a twenty-year sentence for doing something he thought was fun and harmless. His court appointed attorney did very little to defend him as he felt that Deon needed to be punished for his actions after reading the police report. He might've had a lighter sentence if he didn't already have a twenty-page long wrap sheet. Crazy D also had to do additional time while in jail because he ended up breaking the jaw of one of the correction officers. Instead of getting out on parole early, he served the complete 20-year bid.

Chapter 8
The Crew

Crazy D never really intended on a life of crime after he got out of prison, but his options were limited and his choices were few. The crime path became natural because of the rejections he received every time he was honest on a job application about his prison record. Even construction companies turned him down for jobs, even though he was willing to work for minimum wage to gain entry into "civilized" society. After getting out of jail, he received a small stipend that only lasted two weeks while he stayed at a shelter. As the money started to run out because he had spent some of it on clothes at the local Goodwill store in Roxbury and a bus pass to go job hunting, he had to devise a new plan for his life. The filthy shelter where he stayed was dirtier than the prison where he spent his last twenty years and he was tired of living with a bunch of people in filth and having someone always telling him what time to get up and what time to go to bed. Crazy D wanted to take charge of his life and there was only one way he knew how to do that.

Armed only with his prison experience, Crazy D was not going to allow one more person to tell him when to go sleep or wake up anymore. While in Prison, he became a great listener. The proud criminals who admitted to their crime in jail didn't mind divulging their criminal tactics, and Crazy D took it all in. He learned from some of the best and worst criminals while in prison. He knew the mistakes to avoid as well as the right way to go about committing a particular crime without getting caught. More importantly, he learned that police are less likely to investigate crimes involving criminals against other criminals.

A couple of his homeys from the pen were dealt the same fate after they came out of prison. It was time for Crazy D to round up his gang of soldiers to form what became known as the Hoodfellas. Crazy D was smart enough to recognize that he didn't need a big crew in order for him to start his new enterprise, all he needed were a couple of tough soldiers that he could trust. His right hand man and best friend was his old cellmate, Short Dawg. Short Dawg stood at about 5ft 6inches but he was huge. He had a 40 bicep, chest stretched out from New York to LA and feared no one. Short Dawg was an up and coming star running back at English High School before he was implicated in a murder that he nothing to do with.

Before he became known as Short Dawg, Eric was a free man who was walking with a group of idiots who decided to play the knock-out game and one of their chosen victims happened to be a professor at Northeastern University. This frail man didn't even stand a chance as he was selected randomly to be the victim of this kid named Lights Out in the crew. The game was very simple: a victim is pointed out and a crew member is called on to knock the victim out with one punch. Short Dawg wasn't even aware of the game until that very day because he had never walked with this group of dudes before. They were all friends but he wasn't into the bullshit that they were into. He had no idea that his life would change in a flash on that day.

After the professor was pointed out, Lights Out walked up behind him and tapped him on the shoulder, as the professor turned his head to see who it was, he was hit with a devastating blow to the temple by Lights Out. Unaware of his own strength and ability at times, Lights Out put a little too much power behind the punch, and it fatally galvanized the professor to the ground and that's all it took for the District Attorney to seek a life sentence for every person walking together that day, because they were classified as a gang. Short Dawg didn't want to be known as a snitch in the hood, so he took the fall for something stupid that he had nothing to do with. By the time he was convinced to come forward to tell the truth, it was already too late because an all white jury found all ten members in that group guilty of second degree murder.

The name Short Dawg was naturally given to Eric because of his height, stature and his fearless attitude while he was locked up. One of the first altercations he was involved in, he sent a man who was almost twice his size to the hospital. The huge giant thought he could eat twice the serving for the day when he ordered Short Dawg to give up his meal to him. "You must have four sets of teeth because you're trying to eat for two men," Short Dawg told him. "Little man think he's tough. We'll see about that after I mop the floor with yo ass," said the confident giant. Before he even had a chance to step to Short Dawg, a hard blow was delivered to his crotch and he whimpered towards the floor. On his knees, barely tall enough to be eye to eye with Short Dawg and screaming in pain as he held his nuts, Short Dawg cold clock the giant across the mouth and sent him cascading to the floor. The whole cafeteria went into hysteria as Short Dawg took control of the situation. He was like a relentless pit bull as he pounded on the man and beat him to a pulp. The whole prison was screaming, "Short Dawg whooped that ass!" and the name just stuck.

Short Dawg and Crazy became best friends and eventual cellmates while they were at Walpole Correctional Institution together. The two of them always had each other's backs and Short Dawg was always the enforcer between the two. Crazy D's crew inside the prison was also made up of this big ass dude named No Neck, a little nerd named, Tweak and a lunatic named Crusher. No Neck got his name from the simple fact that his neck disappeared because he had gotten so huge from lifting heavy weights. He was 6ft 4 inches tall and weighed 290 lbs. He was sent to the pen for killing his sister's boyfriend. His sister was dating this dude for a while, but the dude was physically abusive to her. The boyfriend would beat up his sister so badly that her whole body would be bruised and she couldn't even hug family members when she came home. Her boyfriend was also a self-proclaimed street thug who vowed to kill her whole family if she ever said anything about the abuse.

It was during a family picnic that No Neck finally discovered what was going on with his sister. Ever since they were children, the family would go to Houghton's Pond in Milton to celebrate 4th of July weekend. It was a short drive from Boston and the family would cook out all day at the pond then jump in the river for a swim. It was always his sister's favorite thing to do. However, this particular 4th of July, instead of wearing her bathing suit, she came all dressed up in Jeans and a shirt, covering her whole body. While horse-playing along with other family members, Joe as he was known to his family before earning the nickname No Neck in jail, picked up his sister and attempted to throw her in the water, but she was wincing in pain as he threw her over his shoulder. The wind blew her shirt exposing her navel area, and that's when Joe noticed the bruises on his sister's body. They were cigarette burns, black and blue marks like she had been tortured and cuts. Upon drilling his sister, she finally revealed to him the abuse she had been suffering at her boyfriend's hands.

What was supposed to be a celebratory, joyous day ended up being a tragic day for Joe and his family. Joe knew exactly where to find his sister's boyfriend because he couldn't leave the block alone even on the fourth of July. Her boyfriend didn't even notice the crack of the bat against his face as Joe hit him repeatedly and stood over him while he screamed "You'll never put your fucking hands on my sister again, punk. I'm gonna kill your fucking ass." And that he did. Joe waited for the cops to show up to arrest him because he already knew what he had done and also knew that he couldn't get away with it.

In jail, Joe bonded with Crazy D instantly. Their love for basketball broke the ice when they first met and they have been friends through their whole prison term. As time went on, Joe became a work-out fanatic, pumping more weight than anybody in the prison. He got so huge over time,

Short Dawg gave him the nickname No Neck while they were in the yard playing basketball one day.

Tweak's path to prison is a little different from all the other guys. He was a victim of his own intelligence. Before Tweak came to prison, he used his government named, which was Ernest. He was one of the brightest kids at Boston Technical high school. He had gotten used to being called a nerd on a daily basis, but he was sick and tired of this one particular kid who kept pointing fingers in his face. One day, while he was sitting in math class trying to take a geometry mid-term exam, this menace named Lenny demanded that he gave him the answers to the test and kept kicking the back of his chair. That torment had been happening all year long and when he complained to the teachers, nothing was ever done about it. That day Ernest got fed up and grew balls the size of an elephant's. "If you kick my chair again I'm gonna fuck you up," he said to the little pest as he got up from his chair. "Shut the fuck up, nerd before I kick your ass in front of the class, nigger," the kid said as his fingers came inches within Ernest's eyeball. He followed it up by spitting in Ernest's face.

There was a limit to how much Ernest would allow a person to degrade him and the kid had reached his limit that day. With brute force, Ernest swung his pencil and stuck it right into the kid's neck, then pulled it out and continued to stab the kid until he fell dead to the floor. No one could believe Ernest's reaction because he had never displayed any type of violent outburst in the past. Even the teacher was too afraid to say anything to him. Ernest was covered in blood with tears rolling down his eyes by the time school security came to take him away in handcuffs. Unfortunately, the menace was a white kid from South Boston and the justice department was not going to let a black boy get away with killing a white boy even if the white boy was in the wrong.

Ernest was found guilty of murder in court, and was sentenced to twenty years in prison. When Ernest first arrived at Walpole, word had gotten out that the scrawny little nerd had killed another kid with a pencil, so people were a little weary of him. He also became the master of weapons while he was in jail as everyone came to him when they needed a weapon for a fight. He earned the nickname Tweak because he was able to tweak anything into a dangerous weapon, even paper. Ernest befriended Crazy D and his crew because they had beef with a white supremacist group from South Boston that was out to get revenge on Ernest. He decided to create enough weapons to arm Crazy D and his crew to go up against the white boys. Once word got out that Tweak was down with Crazy D's crew, the white boys backed fearing that a brawl might escalate to the brink of death for many of them.

Out of everyone in the crew, Crusher was the most violent and dangerous one, but he always needed direction before he acted. Crusher was that kid that should've been in a special class since he started school, but his mother fought hard to keep him in mainstream classes because she refused to believe that her son was disabled. There was nothing abnormal about Crusher when he was a child, but he had a hard time getting along with other children, and his attention span was very short. Named Howard by his mother at birth, Crusher was a premature tiny baby who grew to be 6ft 3inches tall by the time he was thirteen years old. A victim of lead paint and subjected to other urban diseases, he stood very little chance of succeeding in mainstream society.

An introvert at a very young age, Howard had difficulties grasping the basics of things. Back then, psychologists hadn't begun to diagnose children with Attention Deficit Hyperactive Disorder and Bipolar, so Howard was able to get through the cracks into mainstream classes at school. Bright in his own way and with a proud mother, Howard was able to fit in the earlier years of his life at school. However, as time progressed, he became a lot more distant and withdrawn from his peers. He found himself watching a lot of kung fu movies and developed a love for the arts. His mother soon enrolled him in karate school and Howard quickly started earning his way up through the ranks. He trained hard and every other week he was earning a new belt by defeating opponent after opponent placed before him.

One day on his way home from school, a group of kids attempted to rob Howard for his brand new

Adidas shell toes. "Kick in your sneakers," one kid told him. Another kid jumped up and hit him behind the head because he towered over most of them. Howard stood firm and said nothing to the kids. "Kick in your sneakers, we said," repeated another kid as he pulled out a knife and held it next to Howard's heart. Howard was fuming inside, but he knew that he could at least take out a couple of the kids. As two of the kids struggled to tackle Howard to the ground to force him on his back, he punched one on the back and dropped him to the ground. The kid with the knife flung the knife at him a couple times but missed. It was almost ten kids against one, but Howard was determined to win the odds stacked against him. With a closed fist and enough anger coming from his heart, he punched one of the kids in the face sending his body flying against a fence that was about fifteen yards away. He was able to disarm the one kid with the knife and Howard went around and stabbed four of the kids to death. By the time the cops arrived, it was a bloody mess. They commanded him to drop the knife to the ground and he wouldn't. Howard was shot in the leg, but not before stabbing one of the officers as he charged toward them during the hold-down. He was taken into custody, charged with assault with a dangerous weapon on the officer, and second-degree murder on the four kids he killed. Because of his age, Howard received a ten-year sentence, but that sentence would increase when he got to prison because he broke the arms of two prison guards during a riot that took place inside the prison.

The "gentle giant" was the reference made to Howard by his fellow inmates, but two guards found it particularly funny to refer to him as "the big dummy." During a riot between prison officials and the inmates over demands made by the inmates to allow them to read "Street Novels," this one guard ordered Howard to lie down on the floor. Any other time, Crusher would have obeyed the guard's command, but the guard was very disrespectful when he said, "Lie down, big dummy," as another guard laughed on. Howard was already on his knee, but he had long enough reach to grab the guard by the arm and broke it off in two without much struggle. As the second laughing guard approached him with his stick in hand, he also grabbed his arm and broke it along with the stick. Crusher was in the process of sodomizing the two guards with their sticks when 2000 volts of electricity was shot into his body from stun gun.

Howard earned the nickname Crusher from his fellow inmates after breaking the arms of the officers with his bare hands. A couple of inmates also felt the wrath of Howard's strength when they tried to punk him when he first arrived at the prison.

However, he was always provoked before he reacted.

   During his prison sentence, Crazy D managed to earn a GED as well as an Associate's Degree in criminal justice at a cost to the taxpayers, but even that couldn't qualify him for a job in a society where so many prejudices and stereotypes towards felons are pervasive. Armed with the knowledge of the law and his natural instincts and abilities, Crazy D was no longer that 17-year-old fool who went to prison with a naïve state of mind. Crazy D went above and beyond to read about what the laws constitute in regards to forming a criminal enterprise. While his goal may have been to get a job when he got out of prison, he was intelligent enough to recognize that the odds were stacked against him and his choices were limited. So it was on to plan B, and he put together a killer crew that was so sick, it would take the US army to take out his group of dedicated soldiers who are determined to eat better than they have ever eaten off these streets.

Chapter 9
History of Self

When Crazy D came out of prison, it was also time for him to do a little research on his family's history. He learned that he came from a long line of hustlers on both his mother's and father's side of the family. His dad never blossomed to anything because he got killed prematurely, but his grandfather was a bootlegger and businessman who provided enough moonshine to the east coast to supply every liquor store from Washington D.C all the way up to Maine. He died prematurely of liver disease because he had also become addicted to the moonshine he was selling.

His grandmother used her beauty to hustle men most of her life, but she also created her own side hustle in the neighborhood. She was the candy lady, the beer lady, the cigarette lady and anything else that people in the projects who were too lazy to walk to the store wanted. Of course, she made a killing selling liquor on Sundays because liquor stores didn't open on Sundays in Boston. She also enjoyed the finer things in life, so it wasn't unusual for her to fly to New York on a weekend to go party and waste a couple of thousand dollars. However, her overindulgence and vice in life brought her world to a halt because of lung cancer. His grandmother was a pack-a-day smoker for most of her life and she died at the tender age of sixty, a year after Crazy D came out of prison. She was the one who schooled him on his family. She knew his dad's side of the family because the families knew one another since way back and she was part of his grandfather's bootlegging operation.

As far as Serena was concerned, Crazy D had seen everything firsthand. He remembered when she wore fur coats, drove a BMW and spoiled him rotten with the best clothes and toys all while being at home. He didn't know what she was hustling, but he definitely knew that she was a hustler. Crazy D could never figure what happened to his mom when he was young, but he was fortunate enough to learn from his grandmother that Wally was the person responsible for her downfall in life. Serena may have had a few screws loose, but she could always explain to her patient mother how Wally beat her silly. At one point, her mother wanted to find Wally and put a bullet in him herself, but he was too connected for her to find him. She also explained to Crazy D how the neighborhood hustlers used and abused Serena for sexual favors and disrespected her in ways that were inhumane. His grandmother still had a sharp memory, so she was able to remember names and faces as described by her daughter. He clearly understood that a hustler was born, and not made. There was no denying his bloodline and Crazy D planned on hustling until he died.

Crazy D was enamored by the stories told by his grandmother and they captivated him. He also understood that most of his family members never left the projects except for his grand father and unlike them; he was not destined to die there. Crazy D had the fervor and determination to use his natural hustling skills to succeed. Consequently, Crazy D had to avoid the pitfalls that the members of his family had fallen victim to, and he understood that. He had to be innovative and smart. Crazy D was determined to change the legacy of his family.

When Crazy D left his grandmother after spending the whole day with her, he had enough information on his family and the history of his mother since he was locked up, to feel secure enough about his place in society, and how to proceed with his new plan in life. Crazy D had become very particular and his every move was calculated.

Chapter 10
Implementing a New Plan

After rounding up the most trusted people he grew to know while he was in prison, Crazy D called a meeting in Franklin Park because the crew didn't have a place to meet just yet. The five friends went in the back woods of Franklin Park near White Stadium and found an inconspicuous spot where they could meet without interruption.

The first order of the meeting was the target market. Just like a boardroom director, Crazy D handed out a 10-page pamphlet to each of his soldiers, outlining his plan to take over the city of Boston and to earn enough cash that would change their lives forever. The guys paid close attention as Crazy D went over every detail of the plan. Inspired by the way the mob operates, Crazy devised a plan to earn close to a million dollars a week during his first month of operation. A lot of people in Boston, Massachusetts seemed to have been eating well, and there was no reason for Crazy D and his crew to be hungry, he thought.

The first order of business was to get weapons. No criminal enterprise can be built without firepower. Tweak was the official high tech dude in the group and was put in charge of coming up with a plan to arm the group, No Neck was named the public information officer on the street, Short Dawg was in charge of security, Crusher was the enforcer and muscle of the group. Crazy D wanted to remain the brain behind the whole operation. After the meeting, each person was aware of his role in the plan to start getting paid and take over the city block by block.

While in jail, Tweak also became a whiz on the computer as well as an expert in alarm systems. There isn't an alarm system out there that he can't break through. With much practice at home, Tweak was able to go into this gun shop in North Adams, Massachusetts and figured out the floor plan and the alarm system used in that shop to secure the place. Since it was a long ride from Boston, Crusher decided to borrow his mother's car for the long trip. His mother was so happy when her only child came home, there was nothing that she would deny him. Since none of the guys had any money when they first started, they decided to rob the biggest Jewish owned liquor store in the hood. The one thing that Crazy D hated the most after he learned about his mother's life after he came out of prison was drugs and alcohol. It was also one of the sacred rules of the crew to never drink or get high. The liquor store was doing nothing but adding to the strife of the community, so it was an easy target.

Tweak was able to disable the alarm system while Crazy D and Short Dawg walked in wearing helmets and motorcycle gear with gloves covering their bodies completely as they robbed the place. Friday night was the busiest night and they knew they could net the most money. After scoping the place for about an hour, Crazy D and Short Dawg decided to make their move when they noticed two winos who were too drunk to tell anything were the only people in the store before closing. Short Dawg and Crazy D both walked up to the counter with a 20-ounce bottle of Sprite in their hands. As the clerk attempted to ring the bottles up, Short Dawg pulled out a Nine-Millimeter automatic handgun and quietly said in a Caucasian accent and tone, "This is a stick-up. Don't panic and nobody will get hurt." The clerk reached for the silent alarm button, but it meant nothing because Tweak had taken care of it. With the barrel of the gun to his face, the clerk quickly cleared out the register and handed $200.00 to Crazy D. "We don't want that, we want what's in the safe," Crazy D told him. "What safe?" the clerk said acting dumb. "The safe that you're gonna open if you don't want your brain splattered against this wall," Short Dawg replied in a short-tempered manner. After cocking the Nine-Millimeter back, the clerk understood how serious Short Dawg was.

Meanwhile, Crazy D kept his eyes on the two winos who were too drunk to even notice what was going on. When Short Dawg re-emerged from the back room, he had a paper bag full of money in his hand. The clerk was left tied up in the back and Short Dawg and Crazy D left the liquor store quietly. When they got outside, they jumped into a Cadillac that Tweak hotwired and drove to Bailey Street where Crusher was waiting for them in his mother's car. On the way to Bailey Street, Crazy D and Short Dawg took off the motorcycle outfit that they had stolen from the Harley Davidson store. No one was on their trail because the cops were looking for two people on motorcycle who were possibly white.

It turned out that the crew only made about ten grand from the robbery, which was more than enough for their lodging. The funny thing about the whole robbery was that Crazy D and Short Dawg used a couple of toy guns to rob the liquor store. Thanks to Toys R Us selling plastic replicas of real guns to kids, the crew was able to make off with some cash before they made it to the destination to get the real guns.

The formulated plan to break into the gun shop overnight was executed without a hitch. Only Tweak, Crazy D and Crusher drove to North Adams to rob the gun shop. They picked that particular gun shop because Tweak had helped drive his nephew to Massachusetts College of Liberal Arts once and he stopped by the gun shop to check it out. It was also safer to rob because it was away from Boston. Tweak spent a couple of days casing the joint before deciding to rob it as well. He knew the floor plan and every intricate detail about the place. The three men decided to stay at a little motel in nearby Adams when they first arrived in the western part of Massachusetts. They spent the whole weekend planning and outlining the robbery. Tweak felt it would be best to cut a hole in the roof of the building to gain entry. After making sure that the alarm system was disabled, the crew went in and cleaned house. They took every type of gun imaginable along with ammunition. They had enough ammunition to last them through a two-year war.

By the time the owner of the place discovered that it had been robbed, Crazy D, Crusher and Short Dawg were resting in Boston. They were careful to allow only Tweak to go in and register for the room and looking as conservative as he could. There was no suspicion because they stayed about 15 miles away from their target. The crew was now armed and ready to make their move. Crazy D knew exactly who his first victims were going to be.

Chapter 11
Set it off

It was no coincidence that the Hoodfellas robbed the Brown family store first. Crazy D had his public information officer, No Neck, do extensive research on the Browns. And it was found out that Mr. Brown was running numbers, had a gambling ring and making big money while using his store as a front. Many gambling addicts were created in the community because this guy had created an underground gambling ring that netted him close to $500,000.00 a week and Crazy D wanted a piece of it. He also delved into Mr. Brown's past and knew that he was definitely a person of interest to him. Mr. Brown also hosted poker games, dice games as well as black jack in his basement. The Hoodfellas were aware of the amount of money that flowed through Mr. Brown's business. It would've been easy for the Hoodfellas to rob the place and make out big on a Friday night, but Crazy D had bigger plans and he understood that a constant cash flow would take him farther. He pretty much secured a $100,000 a week verbal contract with the Browns. They also took twenty thousand dollars in cash that Mr. Brown had hidden in his vault. Everything was going according to planned and based on the first score, the crew should be living like fat cows in no time. No more shelter life, no more going hungry and definitely no more wearing tight ass, outdated clothes. However, before they could start popping the champagne, Mr. Brown and his security goons wanted to settle the score.

Since Mr. Brown's business was operating illegally, he couldn't call the cops to report the robbery because he didn't want the heat on him, but he was also not going to take that kind of loss. "Look, I don't know who the fuck this guy thinks he is and I really don't give a fuck, but I want his head. The first person who brings his head back will get a hundred thousand dollars from me," Mr. Brown said as he addressed his security team, made up of some of the hardest dudes he could find in the hood, and these guys were loyal to him because he paid them well. The whole security crew dressed in black and wore sunglasses like they were the secret service. There was a total number of ten men and each of them would lay down his life for Mr. Brown because Mr. Brown was pretty much feeding their families.

Unbeknownst to Mr. Brown, Crazy D was not a reactionary man. He was proactive and he already knew that Mr. Brown was going to send his men after his crew. Mr. Brown had called the meeting with his security team a day after the incident with Crazy D, but Crazy D had already paid a couple of soldiers recruited by his information officer to keep watch on Mr. Brown twenty-four hours a day, alternating shifts between them. While Mr. Brown's security crew was meeting in the basement, the two soldiers notified No Neck and the Hoodfellas were ready to take action.

Tweak was able to hotwire a Chevy Suburban and the crew packed into it with their loaded semi automatic weapons. Uzis, Tech nines and Machine Guns were the weapons of choice, and every single weapon had silencers with infrared. Mr. Brown's security team didn't even have a chance to react as they each were taken out while walking out of Mr. Brown's store. The head of security was the only person who had a chance to even fire his weapon because he held one of the dead bodies in front of him as he backed up in the store. The whole assassination went smoothly and quietly. All five men stood on the other side of the Suburban with their weapons loaded and aimed at the front of the store. About nine members of the security team were allowed to make their way out of the store before Crazy D ordered his firing squad to take them out. Nothing was heard as bullets pierced the hearts of all the men with the silencers keeping the noise to a minimum. Not even Mr. Brown was aware that his goons had been taken out until his head of security ran back inside for cover. However, it would only be momentary for him as Crazy D chased him down and put ten shells in his gut and head.

It was a bloody mess, but the crew was very swift in their cleaning efforts. While Crazy went back inside to discuss a new business plan with Mr. Brown, his crew was loading up the Suburban with the dead bodies. "Look, since you no longer have a security team for your business, I decided to provide one of my own at a cost to you. This operation is gonna continue because I don't want you messing with my money, but the terms have changed drastically. From now on, 80% of this operation is mine and my security men will make sure that you never cross the line again," Crazy D told Mr. Brown as he stood there shaking in shock. Mr. Brown's men were taken out so swiftly, he couldn't believe it. "I know the kind of money that is made here on a weekly and monthly basis, and we're gonna increase business by 200% under my leadership. If you as much think about crossing me again even in your dreams, you better wake up and call me to apologize. We can't afford to shut down this operation and you don't have to worry because my men have already taken care of the mess. Your job is to keep business as normal as possible for your clients and just explain to them you have new security because the last crew was stealing from you." Crazy D laid out his plan to Mr. Brown and left no room for negotiation.

After leaving a few of his men behind to secure his place in Mr. Brown's establishment, he gave orders to his men to torch the Chevy Suburban so no trace of the dead bodies could be found. The truck was taken to an abandoned field and burned to a crisp. The human remains were never identified and Mr. Brown knew that Crazy D was serious about his business.

Chapter 12
The Turning Point

All Crazy D wanted was a job at the grocery store, but Mr. Brown was mean and condescending when he walked in the store to inquire about a job. A gentleman in a suit was conversing with Mr. Brown when Crazy D walked and respectfully waited for his turn to ask if Mr. Brown was hiring. "Can't you see that I'm conducting business?" Mr. Brown screamed at Crazy D after he asked if he was hiring. "I'm sorry, sir. I just want a job," Crazy D replied. "Your dumb ass needs to learn how to approach people. You can't be walking into my establishment like you know me. Get the fuck outta my store," he yelled at Crazy for no reason while he tried to show off for the man in the suit. It would've been easy for Crazy D to let the incident go, but he became curious when he saw Mr. Brown later that day driving around the hood in a convertible Bentley. That's when he began his investigation on Mr. Brown and he knew there was some type of illegal activity going on in the store.

Mr. Brown brought it on himself when he decided to drive his Bentley to his store that day. Crazy D was able to find out that the gambling ring created by Mr. Brown had been operating for the last three years and more money was coming out of that store than they sold in goods everyday. Before he even brought his crew together, he mapped out his different targets for his big payday. Crazy D was relentless as he went by the store at every hour of the day to monitor the activities. He noticed when the dirty cops picked up their security money, he knew when the city counselor had lunch with Mr. Brown and when envelops and money were exchanged for favors. He knew that Mr. Brown was very connected and he knew the risk that he was taking before he decided to make his move against Mr. Brown. It was an uphill battle, but he had Brown cornered.

No successful gambling ring can last in the hood for more than a year without the person running the ring having some type of political and police connection to some higher power in government. Crazy D learned from his grandmother that Tremaine Brown was the reason why his mother's life took a turn for the worse, but more than that, she also told him how Mr. Brown turned to a snitch after he was caught by the feds for drug trafficking. He was offered a deal to set up his suppliers and the Feds made it look like he was taken down along with the crew. While most people he snitched on got twenty-five to life, Mr. Brown walked away with a two-year sentence and a license to do whatever the hell he wanted in the hood, except sell drugs. There was no negotiating the sale of drugs. Being the natural hustler that he was, he decided to start running numbers and that grew to a full gambling ring with Black Jack tables, Poker table and Roulette tables in the basement of his business. He could've called it Brown's little casino.

The local officials didn't really give a fuck that he was causing a different kind of strife in the hood, turning people to addicts with a dollar and a dream. The more money he made, the bigger his operation grew and the more officials he got on his payroll. Even the mayor benefited from his illegal gambling activity through his big donations funneled through his grocery store, so Mr. Brown was protected and connected. Crazy D was aware of all that and it was a risk he was willing to take.

With a hatred for corrupt authority and a desire to get revenge for his mother while pursuing a posh lifestyle, Crazy D set out to take over Tremaine's operation as well as another man whose illegal escort service was of high interest to him as well. The escort service was an even bigger score, but it would prove harder to penetrate than the illegal gambling ring of Tremaine. The playboy Mansion has nothing on the Webster mansion better known as the WW spot. The Webster mansion was the place where politicians, high rollers, professional athletes, CEOs and other notables went to get their sexual needs met discreetly. That operation was a multi-million dollar operation weekly and Crazy D had his eyes on it.

Chapter 13
Webster's mansion

The mansion itself was built like a fortress and security swarmed around the place like the queen of England, the United States President and the Saudi King all lived in that mansion together. The fifteen-inch thick and seven-foot high wall built around the mansion was enough to deter the most patient and determined of men to say forget it, but Crazy D wasn't the average man. He had learned patience while he was in prison, and understood that with time everything was possible. After watching the movie, Shawshank Redemption, that belief was reinforced even more. Tim Robbins' character was the perfect motivation as he was a captive man with nothing but time on his hand and the enduring task of breaking out an impenetrable prison wall with tools that could've driven him insane, but his patience outweighed the task. Penetrating those walls would prove difficult for Crazy D and his crew. They wouldn't have to literally penetrate the walls as in the movie, but they would have to find a way to fit in so they could gain entry into that "high class" group of people.

Diplomats, who used their diplomatic status to pull favors for Mr. Webster whenever he needed something, often, visited the Webster mansion. It was normal for twenty to thirty limousines to pull in and out of the mansion daily. The guards at the front gate carried high- powered riffles, automatic weapons as well as K-9 dogs in case there was any imminent threat.

Behind the mansion walls, women paraded in thongs, bras and high heels. Women of all nationalities and race earned their living at the 125-room mansion. Dignitaries were treated to luxury suites while the regular politicians had their ways with women in luxurious rooms with the women of their choice. The men who visited the mansion came from all levels of government, local, state and federal. Senators, congressional representatives, district attorneys and judges all found pleasure behind the mansion wall. Unlike Hugh Heffner's Playboy mansion, Webster's was a well-known secret. A secret to those who had never been there, but well known to those who frequented the place for sex and pleasure.

Only a few minutes from Boston, Webster's mansion was hidden in the back hills of Milton on a private five-acre estate. The place was bought with money funneled illegally through a legitimate corporation set up by a greedy lawyer who got more than enough of his share of the illegal drug money that bought the place. A connected man, the lawyer was able to introduce Mr. Webster to all of his powerful associates and he won them over with his charisma and charm. Fundraisers were held at the mansion as well as catered weddings for the rich and famous, all in secret. Mr. Webster realized that he could make more money selling sex to those horny men who were tired of their boring wives most of the time, and that's how the business was changed even though it was still registered as a catering hall.

Women were discreetly recruited from every college campus in Boston. The kind of money they were offered was hard to pass up. Mr. Webster sent his recruiters in limousines to the hottest clubs and these women were treated to the best champagne and wine offered by the establishments. One by one these women were recruiting their friends and telling them how they could earn as much as twenty thousand dollars a week entertaining politicians and other powerful, rich men. Mr. Webster wanted to take on the persona of Hugh Heffner, but he chose not to sleep with any of the Webster Girls, as they were called. He married this woman who was about fifteen years his junior and she was in charge of the day-to- day operation of the girls. Most of the girls had no idea that the cell phones given to them by Mrs. Webster were tapped and also had trackers on them. It was important for them to keep tabs on every single girl that worked at the mansion because of the risk of exposure involved. Mr. Webster ensured his clients complete discretion and he made sure that he delivered on his promise.

There was a situation where one of the girls started talking to friends about an encounter she had with a well-known politician at the mansion and she was found decapitated the next day. The girls were never allowed to drive directly to the mansion. They were picked up by Mr. Webster's drivers and taken to the mansion when they had to report to work everyday. Mr. Webster was the only person who determined when work was over and the girls had no choice but to wait to be driven home. All of the clients knew that they had to keep their mouth shut about the goings-on at the mansion. All the limousine drivers were trusted men of Mr. Webster who earned six-figure salaries, and they made sure they took the most complicated route to the mansion in order to keep the location a secret. The one time one of them made the mistake of talking to a friend about the possible location of the mansion and what went on there, Mr. Webster's hired guns killed her and her friends. Everybody who worked for Mr. Webster had his/her phone and car wiretapped because he trusted no one. A membership at Webster's mansion was for life, as well as employment. This man had built an organization like the FBI. He kept tabs on every single person that worked for him.

Chapter 14

A Lucky Break

Since Crazy D was now banking mad money every week, he could afford to spend some time focusing on Webster's mansion. Everything he had heard up 'til then was rumored. There was no proof that the mansion actually existed. However, he wanted to find out. Crazy D's prison sentence also gave him the opportunity to learn how to be a chameleon. He could switch from thug to corporate like it was nothing. The first move was to establish a new identity as the owner of a start-up Dotcom company out of Semi Valley, California. He was an overnight success and he was going to parlay his new identity to gain entry into the mansion. Actually, Crazy D caught a lucky break one day when he met this young woman named Cindy at a club on Lansdowne Street in Boston.

She was a beautiful white girl from Worcester who attended Boston College. She was able to attend Boston College on a full academic scholarship. When she first got to the school, she didn't fit in with the rest of the rich white kids on campus. She lied about her background and the fact that she lived in a trailer park in Worcester. The first person in her family to go to college, Cindy was determined not to return to the trailer park. Opportunity came knocking one day when she met one of Mr. Webster's associates. She was ecstatic at the opportunity to earn so much money, and she figured it was a way to move her mother out of the trailer park. She was pampered that evening and received VIP treatment like a royal princess, it was something she had never experienced before and it was a high she never wanted to end.

A meeting was set up, and Cindy was hired immediately by the house madam. On a scale of 1-10, Cindy was definitely a perfect 10. She was a cross between Cindy Crawford and Angelina Jolie. Sexy in every way, the madam knew that Cindy was going to make the mansion a lot of money. A salary of twenty thousand dollars a week was offered to her and she couldn't refuse it. "Cindy, let me tell you something," the madam said to her, "Right now you're probably sleeping with a bunch men because you like them and you get nothing out of it. How about you start sleeping with men and get rewarded handsomely for it? You can make a lot of money here." After a forty-five minute meeting, Cindy was convinced it was the right move for her. However, the one thing that the madam failed to reveal to her was the fact that her employment was until her beauty faded, at which time, her life would be over as well. No one lived to talk about the mansion.

That was the rule, a rule that Cindy was unaware of from the start.

When Crazy D met Cindy he had no idea that she was connected to the mansion, but he soon found out after she had a couple of drinks in her. Dressed as the successful baller that most women yearn to meet, Crazy D exuded confidence, wealth and charm while wearing an expensive virgin wool, tan Armani suit, brown suede Gucci shoes, brown suede Gucci belt to match and a white linen shirt in the middle of summer. The aroma of his cologne pulled Cindy right in as she made her way to the bar near Crazy D. He had left the VIP section to check out the rest of the club for a few minutes. "What's that cologne you're wearing?" she asked. "Armani Code," he answered. "It's very becoming," she flirted. "What are you drinking?" he asked. "I'll have a glass of Dom Perignon" she said. Crazy D immediately ordered a bottle of Dom Perignon and then asked the bartender to put it on his tab. While conversing for about forty-five minutes and a few glasses of champagne later, Cindy started to reveal her pain to Crazy D.

"My best friend just got killed and I think I know who did it," she said. "How did your friend die?" Crazy D asked. "I don't really know but I think my boss had something to do with it," she said. "Why would your boss want to kill your friend?" he asked. "Well, I work at this mansion where I make a lot of money and I brought my friend in to work there with me after getting it approved by the madam. She liked my friend's pictures and she wanted me to bring her in for work. My friend met me at my house where the driver picked us up. From the very beginning, my boss made it clear to us that we couldn't talk about the place, but my friend couldn't keep her mouth shut. One day after telling her friends how she was earning a living because they couldn't understand how she could afford her luxurious lifestyle, she turned up dead in the Charles River. The reason why I think my boss might have had something to do with it is because she called and told me that she was talking to some friends about what we do. I immediately became suspicious." Crazy D was more of a listener when he needed to be and he was all ears as she spilled her guts out while under the influence of alcohol. "What is it exactly that you do that is so dangerous and secretive?" Crazy D asked. She looked around before answering him, as she was becoming a lot more cautious than before. She also learned to leave the company cell phone in the car when she was out on personal business. "I can't talk about that right now," she said. It took but five minutes for her to whisper in Crazy D's ears that she was horny and would rather finish the conversation back at his place.

By now, Crazy had secured a two-bedroom loft apartment right in the heart of downtown Boston. His two security officers sat in the car the whole night to make sure that Crazy D was safe. He had already become enemy number one when he decided to take over Mr. Brown's business, so he made sure he was safe at all times. Crazy D jumped in a black Chevy Suburban and had his security guard drop him off at his pad with Cindy. She was too drunk to drive her car, so she left it in the parking lot downtown. While in a drunken state, Cindy ran down every detail of what she did at the mansion and how she feared that she would never be able to leave the place unless she was willing to face her own death. First, Crazy D had to please this horny white chick.

His Sean John boxers came off easily as Cindy made her way down his crotch to take his ten inches in her mouth. Her lips galloped around his dick like a Trojan horse in the battlefield. An oral expert since she was a junior in high school, Cindy deep throat Crazy D's dick slowly while slobbing and jerking him off. "Damn baby, you really know how to suck a dick," Crazy D whispered. "You like that?" she asked. "Yes, I do," he answered like he was at the alter answering a priest. The dick sucking skills of a white woman can sometimes fool a man into thinking she's worth marrying. As Cindy worked her razor tongue around Crazy D's dick, he grabbed the back of her neck for comfort. "Suck that dick, baby," he exclaimed. Cindy's voracious appetite for his big black dick was endless and she wanted to ride him. After wrapping himself in a Trojan condom, the pinkness of her white dripping pussy was tantalizing. She got on top of him while facing the mirrored wall and started to ride him up and down. He could see her pussy sliding up and down his dick and that turned him on even more.

The fine hairs on her pussy were soaked as her wetness took over his dick. "You have a huge cock, daddy. Give it to me," she begged. Crazy D thrust himself harder as she came down to meet his hard strokes. His dick was damn near traveling up her back, but she loved every minute of it. "I want you to get on your stomach," he ordered. Cindy effortlessly rolled on her stomach with very little ass to get a black man's blood pumping, but it didn't matter because Crazy D was already hard and it was all about getting his nut off. He glided his dick in Cindy's pussy while inserting his index finger in her ass. He pushed harder and she begged for more. "I want you to fuck me in my ass," she requested. With a little bit of lubrication from his saliva, Crazy D found his dick sliding with ease into Cindy's asshole. "Oh yes, fuck me!" she screamed. With all ten inches fully erect inside Cindy's ass, Crazy D went to work. "You like this dick, huh? Take that!

Take that!" he screamed as he forcefully tore up Cindy's ass. "I'm about to come, daddy," she said to him like he was a customer at the mansion, but her orgasm was 100% real, not fake like those she pretended to have while working at the mansion. As she screamed in ecstasy, Crazy D increased the motion of his strokes for a back shot. Within minutes, the condom came off and Cindy was swallowing every drop of his cum with ease.

After sexing Cindy mandingo style, Crazy D vowed to help her get revenge on her boss for killing her best friend. Crazy D also had an ulterior motive because he was seeking his own revenge on this man who had done too much wrong in his eyes to even deserve to live. The owner of the mansion had become enemy number one to Crazy D a week after he got out of prison. He had learned too much about the man to let him go about his business without paying his debt to him.

It may have been a coincidence, but Cindy was more than happy to have met Crazy D. She knew him by the name of Deon and shortly thereafter, she found herself falling deeper and deeper for Deon's long strokes. Not one to be affected by coochie, Crazy D focused on his goal to get to Webster's mansion. Cindy also became the center of Deon's life because she was the vehicle that would drive him to his destination.

Chapter 15
Tremaine Brown

"I ain't no punk. I ain't gonna let these bastards come to my house and think that they're gonna take over an operation that took me years to build," Tremaine said to his wife. "Back when I was hustling drugs, I killed more people than these bastards ever seen alive and they think they can just walk into my business and take it over? They better think again," he continued with his rant, trying to convince himself that he could stand up to the Hoodfellas. His wife never uttered a word because she knew that her husband was more talk than action. Word on the street was that Tremaine was a chump, but he always had enough money to pay for protection and muscle. When he was selling drugs, he was robbed more times than the local bank. Stick-up kids had his number on speed dial.

Whenever someone robbed him for his signature chain he was so proud to wear, he would go and get the exact same chain to conceal the fact that he had been robbed. He was always too scared to retaliate, but he'd have the whole world believe that he had the heart of a lion. Tremaine was about his money and he didn't care what he had to do to get it.

Once, one of his major distributors set him up. A deal was made to secure five keys of pure white snow at twenty-two grand a key by one of his usual dealers, when Tremaine got to the meeting spot, a stick-up kid pulled out a gun, put it to his head and threatened to end his life. He wet his pants that day while begging for his life. The kid got away with the drugs and robbed Tremaine of his jewelry and money. When he called the dealer to find out if he was set up, the dealer told him that he didn't like his punk ass and that he was lucky that he was still breathing. Tremaine hung up the phone while shaking in his pants because he knew the dealer was a certified killer that could take his life without a second thought. He wore a bulletproof vest and walked around with bodyguards for almost a year after that incident. He never tried to recover his drug, jewelry or money because he was too scared. He charged it all to the game. The dealer no longer wanted to deal with Tremaine because he had found a better price from another distributor.

Tremaine couldn't understand why he was targeted by Crazy D, but it was time for him to at least attempt to be a man. In his mind, he had everything planned out. The next time he saw Crazy D, he was gonna walk up to him with guns blazing and just smoke him like a scene out of a bad gangster movie. The scene kept playing over and over in his head. He carried two loaded Nine-Millimeter revolvers with him to work everyday hoping to come face to face with Crazy D. As he wished, Crazy D came to collect the money early on a Friday and Tremaine came face to face with him. "You think your punk ass can just come in here talking about you're taking over my shit," he said with one gun drawn to Crazy D's face while the other gun is kept on two of the security guards at the place. The lack of confidence was evident in his voice. "I see you're tryna grow some balls," Crazy D said without batting an eye. "I'mma blow your fucking head off, bitch" Tremaine yelled out. While losing control over his emotion, Tremaine never saw the massive hands of No Neck coming across his right eye with enough power to put a dent on the fender of a Hummer. He went crashing to the floor, losing consciousness. By the time he came to, Crazy D had him tied up to a chair with gasoline poured all over his body and kept flicking a lighter in his hands. The fear of being burned alive gripped the mind of Tremaine and he broke down like a bitch.

Tears and groans could be heard throughout the basement as Tremaine begged Crazy D to spare his life. "I'm only gonna say this once and I want you to listen clearly: If you ever try to cross me ever again, you will have your balls for breakfast, your toes and fingers for lunch and your eyeballs and dick for dinner. Furthermore, I think you have a hearing problem, so I'm gonna make sure that you use your one good ear to always listen to what I have to say to you," Crazy D said with authority. Tremaine didn't fully understand the complete statement, but he knew that it was the last time he was going to ever walk around with two ears. Crazy D pulled a knife out of his back pocket and with one swift hand stroke, Tremaine's left ear fell to the ground leaving the side of his head bleeding. "Ugh!" he screamed but he was quickly gagged when No Neck placed his hands over Tremaine's mouth while Crazy D poured alcohol over the wound. The fear in Tremaine's face was enough to convince Crazy D that he would never in his dreams try anything like that again. Crazy D wanted to be fair, so he ensured Tremaine that he had a job for life as the front man of the organization, but the Hoodfellas now owned his whole enterprise and his salary was a nonnegotiable thousand dollars a week until Crazy D deemed it necessary to shut down the operation. The Bentley, the big house in Stoughton, Massachusetts and the convertible Benz now belonged to the Hoodfellas enterprise and Tremaine had to pay a thousand dollar monthly fee to have access to them.

Crazy D wanted to take complete control of Tremaine's life because he knew that a coward could any day take advantage of an opportunity because of fear. He never underestimated his Tremaine because he had taken over Tremaine's livelihood. Tremaine was being watched 24hrs a day from the time Crazy D decided he was going to take over the business, and every street associate of Tremaine's was killed by the Hoodfellas one by one. Tremaine was on his own and there was nothing he could do about it. Crazy D knew he couldn't get rid of Tremaine because he had all the contacts to keep the operation going, but he wanted to make sure that there was no way out for Tremaine as well.

Tremaine had one more trick up his sleeve and he wanted to make sure it didn't bring about his demise. The two corrupted officers who have been on his payroll since the inception of his illegal gambling ring never saw any interruption in their pay because Crazy D knew that he needed them for protection and to keep a close eye on the police department in case of a takedown. Tremaine continued to act like he was the man, but the cops grew suspicious because he wasn't his jovial, cocky self around them anymore. Afraid to speak at the establishment, he signaled the cops to meet him away from the store later on. Crazy D could monitor Treamine's conversation because his cell phone was tapped, but he couldn't monitor his text messages. It took Crazy D a long time to figure out how to use text messaging because he was years removed from technology before he went to prison. One of the officers received a text from Tremaine asking him to meet up later on at a local bar. The officers also found it odd that all of Tremaine's security staff were new men. The bandage around Tremaine's ears was also a dead give away, but the dirty cops couldn't react right away because they still had their careers to worry about. They probably made more money illegally than they did legally, but it was the legal gig that allowed them to make the illegal money, and they couldn't risk that.

Tremaine was no fool. He knew that his every move was being monitored by Crazy D and his gang of Hoodfellas. Trying to outsmart Crazy D was going to be a task. Though Crazy D had been to Tremaine's house, he never discovered the escape route that Tremaine had specifically built with his own hands in case the heat ever came down on him. He didn't just own his house, but he also owned the house next door. Tremaine was able to sneak downstairs in the basement through his escape route to go meet with the dirty cops unnoticed. When he arrived at the bar, he found the two detectives sitting at the bar in plain clothes. "What's going on, Tre? You didn't seem like yourself today, and what's up with all this new security you got in there?" said Steve Flynn while his partner, Ray Bratton looked on. These dirty Irish cops were shaking down every illegal enterprise in the city of Boston and were raking in over five million dollars a year between them. It was in their best interest to make sure that Tremaine wasn't being violated, but they had no idea what kind of adversary they were about to face in the Hoodfellas. "I need you guys to help me get rid of these guys who are practically trying to take over my operation," Tremaine told them. "How does that affect us? We're still getting paid. Our job is to protect the business, not the individual. We're not trying to meddle in anyone's beef," said Bratton. Tremaine didn't really know how to respond to that, so he thought about it and was trying to come with an offer to the cops that they couldn't refuse.

Tremaine started to see greed in the eyes of the cops and he was trying to figure out a way to persuade them that he was more important to them than the business, and without him there would no longer be a gambling ring. Completely aware of the fact that his stake in the business no longer existed, without going into too much detail, Tremaine offered the dirty cops half of his monthly net profits so they can get rid of Crazy D and his crew. The money sounded great, but these cops weren't really hurting for dough. However, greed is the root of all evil as it relates to money. Before deciding to accept Tremaine's offer, the two cops wanted to find out every bit of information on the Hoodfellas as possible. The only information Tremaine provided them was Cray D's name because that's all he had. There was no gang affiliation on the street and the name Hoodfellas was only known amongst the five members. It was gonna be a task for the two dirty cops to learn everything they could about Crazy D and his gang in their own time because it was a side gig. They set out to watch the gang and see what they were all about.

Meanwhile, Tremaine never got the relief that he was looking for as the cops told him they needed a week to make their decision. Still, he was betting on the cops busting Crazy D so he could go back to running his business as usual. Tremaine's hands were tied and he knew that if his next move against Crazy D wasn't successful he was a dead man.

Chapter 16
Dirty Cops

Steve Flynn and Ray Bratton met at the police academy. After introducing themselves to each other, the two became friends instantly. Having shared the similar background of being raised in the two most racist parts of Boston during the 70's and 80's, the two had a lot in common. Steve Flynn was born and raised in South Boston where they hurled rocks and racial epithets at elementary school aged kids and took pride in their racist attitudes, while Ray Bratton lived on the other side where things weren't much different. Black people couldn't walk through Charlestown or South Boston after dark during the 70's and 80's. It's not as if these racist bastards were tough or anything, but they would load up a truck of ten white boys with baseball bats to go after one black person. Black kids felt the wrath of these ignorant bastards for decades before bussing was introduced in Boston. Not to say there's any racial harmony there now, but Boston has come a long way. However, those racist sentiments that Bratton and Flynn grew up with never went away.

Upon graduating from the police academy, Flynn and Bratton became partners. Whether they were ever good patrolmen on the streets of Boston, no one would ever know, but they moved through the ranks pretty rapidly. After just five years on the force, they both became detectives. Because they both were assigned to the precinct on Blue Hill Ave. in Mattapan, they had to meddle in the daily lives of Black folks and many victims suffered as a result.

While patrolling the streets of Boston for five years, Bratton and Flynn harassed enough young black men to get kicked off the force. Black men in the hood were subjected to maltreatment and malfeasance whenever these two knuckleheads were called to a scene. There was a particular incident that involved two young men screaming at each other, but with no punches thrown in Mattapan Square. When the two officers arrived at the scene, they tried as much as they could to infuriate the two young men. "You niggers don't know how to stay outta trouble, do you?" said Flynn "Who the fuck are you calling a nigger?" said one of the young men angrily. "It looks like we have a ballsy little nigger on our hands," said Bratton. As people started to gather around, the two cops refrained from using the N word, but they never stopped their relentless effort to get the two young men to react to them so they could place them under arrest. Bratton decided to search the young man who responded to them first, and upon his search, he found a joint in the kid's pocket. An argument ensued and the young man ended up with a police stick upside his head and in the hospital with a broken jaw, while the other one was pepper sprayed for trying to keep the cops from beating the young man.

That was the only blemish on their record because the case received a little scrutiny from the media. However, they had been beating up young men in the hood from the time the two loose canons were set on the street. Shortly after their probationary period was over, Bratton and Flynn started shaking down the local drug dealers. Each time they caught a dealer with drugs and money; the money was theirs and the dealer had to give them half the money they would make selling the drugs after they let them go. There was no honor among thieves and the drug dealers were starting to feel the financial pain of Bratton and Flynn's ways. When one of the drug dealers threatened to go to the authorities if the duo didn't stop shaking them down, he received a bullet to the skull and a dirty gun in his right hand in a gun battle that he appeared to have had with himself. Words about the drug dealer spread like wildfire and that pretty much cemented Bratton and Flynn's reputation as ultimate pimps of the drug dealers. So much money was being made by the duo they hired street look-outs to make sure the dealers weren't talking to any other cops.

Tremaine became a victim of the duo when he was caught with twenty kilos of cocaine in the back of his Mercedes after being pulled over by the duo. Upon an illegal search of his car, the drug was found along with half a million dollars. The money was kept and he was let go after a deal of $500,000.00 was worked out. Tremaine didn't hesitate to accept the deal because he faced more than twenty years in prison if they took him to jail. However, the cops got greedy and wanted a bigger share of Tremaine's drug empire. He decided to leave the drug game alone and started to run numbers until the duo caught up with him again. They knew that Tremaine was a hustler and there was nothing else he could do to support the lavish lifestyle he had grown accustomed to. He soon found himself paying the cops for looking the other way and the way they put it to him, "You either pay us or we bring down your operation. You know the procedure, and if you open your mouth to the authorities you will be dealt the same fate as your drug dealing friend who was found in the abandoned house with a bullet to his skull." Tremaine already knew it wasn't a threat because the two cops were known to most of the street hustlers.

Bratton and Flynn knew from the time they decided to join the Boston Police force they were not going to be model cops. They were the biggest haters in the hood, especially when they saw a brother driving any type of high-end luxury car. The fifty-thousand dollar salary they earned was not enough for the lifestyle they dreamed about. While they became stars in the police department because of their connections instead of valor and dedicated service, they also developed vices. There was no difference between the pair and the drug dealers they were trying to take down. Flynn was the flashier of the two. He used the fact that he lived with his crooked parents as a front to justify the seventy-thousand dollar Mercedes Benz that he drove. He also bought houses, boats and vacation homes all in the name of his parents. Flynn had more than his share of women. He was the star of South Boston. Every woman wanted him and he slept with almost every woman he could. Lavish trips to Vegas were the norm for him and his girlfriends. Foxwoods Casino became his second home and a second justification for his lavish lifestyle. He had everyone believe that he was an expert in poker and that he won regularly at the casino in Foxwoods in Connecticut. Flynn thought he had everything under control.

Bratton led a modest life but he had a mistress in addition to his wife and two children. While he lived in a moderate three-bedroom and two-bath house with his wife in Charlestown, he helped his mistress purchase a two-bedroom penthouse condominium in downtown Boston. According to his wife, he spent long hours working over time to earn extra cash. Sure, he did that, but not enough to afford a million dollar penthouse. His wannabe model girlfriend worked odd jobs as a waitress. She was as gorgeous as a woman could be and turned more heads than Drew Barrymore. Bratton was proud of himself whenever he was out with Laura, his mistress girlfriend. He never hid the fact that he was married from Laura, but he lied about being unhappy at home. Bratton was devoted to his family and loved his wife dearly, but he lacked dick control. His mistress was nothing more than a high price ho who wanted to live the high life and Bratton was stupid enough to provide it for her. Over time, she had him wrapped around her finger. Though he wanted to come off as threatening and tough, she was never afraid of him.

In reality, Bratton and Flynn were nothing more than two criminals with a legal badge and a gun tormenting people and extorting them out of their money. Crazy D had them figured out and he devised a plan to deal with them in case they ever went against him. Bratton and Flynn may have thought that their position with the police department would give them access to Crazy D and his crew and the luxury of investigating them at will, but Crazy D had his own investigator within his own crew ready to expose the two cops for the criminals that they were. The badge never really solidified anything against the Hoodfellas.

Chapter 17
Keeping His Eyes on the Prize

Crazy D had come, conquered Tremaine Brown's business, and had his public information officer pull more dirt on everyone who ever visited the gambling ring from the time he took it over. Every businessman, politician, police officer, hooker, drug dealer and baller had a personal file created by Tweak. He had set up high tech surveillance on the two crooked cops and even recorded them while they were being paid off a few times. The hidden cameras these days are so small, a diamond-encrusted medallion may just be a camera and that's what Tweak used to get footage of Bratton and Flynn. There's no need to wear a wire anymore when a small hidden camera can do the trick.

The money the Hoodfellas were making was a lot more than they ever made since coming out of prison, but Crazy D was looking at things on a grander scale. The Webster mansion was where the real money was being made and he needed to find entry there as soon as possible. It was gonna be easier said than done. Most of the clients who visited the mansion were invited either by a visiting patron, or Mr. Webster himself would extend a personal invitation to them.

Deon continued to wine and dine Cindy until she started catching feelings so strong for him that she felt the need to speak to him three to four times a day. And Deon played right along even though he was annoyed by her most of the time. Convincing her not to allow her friend to die in vain was always at the forefront of his conversation and finding a way out of the mansion for her. Deon made promises of marriage and a family life with Cindy and acted as if her profession didn't bother him. "Baby, we gotta get you outta that line of work you're in. I can see us with the white picket fence, big house, two children and a dog. That's what I see in our future," he would tell her after tearing her ass up with his mandingo strokes. "I don't know how I'm gonna leave that job because I don't want to die," she'd respond. "I'll take care of that. I just need to be able to get into the mansion," he told her. "I'll see what I can do," she assured him.

A few weeks after meeting Deon, Cindy finally realized that the mansion was all about making money. She went to her madam and told her about this rich millionaire that she met, but she wanted him to become a client in-house because she didn't want to get involved with him personally. Deon played the role of a millionaire perfectly. He changed his attire from thug to complete professional. He spent a lot of money on tailor-made suits and even rode around in a chauffeured Mayback driven by one of his men. The Mayback set him back three hundred and fifty thousand dollars, but it was for a grander cause and the crew understood.

Unlike Cindy who tricked at the mansion for money, Deon was more interested in the complete operation of the mansion. After dishing out $50,000 for a membership, Deon finally gained access to the mansion. It took some work, but a bogus website and a fake business license did the trick. The people at Webster's mansion tried as much as they could to dig into Deon's background, but they came up with information that Tweak wanted them to find. As a computer genius, Tweak was able to generate fake links about Deon and his business whenever a search was generated from the Webster mansion through GOOGLE. Satisfied with the information they acquired, the mansion willingly welcomed their worst enemy into the house. Everything about the mansion was presidential and the women were as fine as they come.

Undeterred by pussy, Deon only asked to be with Cindy when he visited the mansion. He was also smart enough to recognize that his every move was being watched because only a fool would believe that there was any privacy at the mansion. Too many politicians in one place is always reason to keep watch over people. The first time Deon got with Cindy he made sure she acted like they were strangers. While trying his best to put on a sexual act, he looked around the room inconspicuously searching for hidden cameras and voice recording devices. While the patrons were free to walk around the common areas in the compound, there were restricted areas as well. Those restricted areas piqued Deon's interest. Armed security walked around the compound in black suits, away from the patrons and Deon was mostly concerned about a free path to the operating room. He wanted to know the day-to-day operation of the mansion as well as its financial interest.

Chapter 18
The Businessman

As a businessman, Deon understood that he had to delegate some of his duties to his fellow officers. The take-over of Mr. Brown's operation was pretty much a done deal as Deon had his hands and his men involved in every aspect of the operation. The two crooked cops were his biggest concerns, but he had to leave them up to Short Dawg to deal with for now. Short Dawg hated those two cops with a passion, but Deon made it clear to him that he was not to allow his emotions to affect his decisions. Short Dawg was under close watch whenever the two cops were around. Deon didn't want him to blow up for no reason. Meanwhile, spending was kept to a minimum and some of the Hoodfellas weren't too happy. As much money as they were making, the fellas wanted a taste of the good life, too. But only Tweak understood and saw the bigger picture. He tried his hardest to convince the rest of the crew to follow the directives of Crazy D, but it was becoming an uphill battle because Crazy D wasn't around to enforce any of his rules. Crazy's D's focus was the big money at the mansion and he knew that he couldn't go on living as an extortionist for the rest of his life. His main goal was to get himself and his crew set for life.

It was difficult for the Hoodfellas not to become disgruntled, because Crazy D was riding around in a Mayback while he ordered them to stick to a basic lifestyle. No one saw the bigger picture like he did, and he was trying his hardest to make sure he delivered on his plan. No one knew Crazy D's plan but him. Taking over Mr. Brown's operation was just the beginning, but Deon wanted more. His dream was to have his own empire and he was willing to die trying to acquire it. Deon wore many hats within his organization. While wearing his businessman hat, Deon knew that the only chance he had to become a legitimate businessman had to come by way of cash. The only way to get the amount of cash that he needed to put his plan in motion was to basically get the biggest business in town, which was the mansion. He knew that the beautiful women at the mansion brought in a lot of money for Mr. Webster and he wanted it all. From a legal standpoint, the mansion was the most illegal operating business in the city, but too many powerful people were involved to bring it down.

Deon lost many nights of sleep trying to come up with a plan that would catapult him to the top. Time was definitely not on his side because his men were growing very impatient and they had no idea that most of the money extorted from Mr. Brown's business was being spent to help Deon front as a businessman. He lied to them about the amount of money they had saved and told them that he was close to making twenty million dollars, which would set them all for life. As a matter of fact, Deon didn't even know where the millions of dollars he guaranteed his men was going to come from.

Deon may not have had a college degree, but he was one of the smartest men that the criminal justice system held captive. The time he spent behind bars afforded him the luxury to craft his skills as an analytical thinker and problem solver. He understood clearly that what the mansion was doing was illegal and there was no way for him to bring it down without the proper plan. He also understood that the amount of cash the mansion generated could not truthfully be reported to Uncle Sam, so some of it had to have been stashed in a safe somewhere. After visiting the mansion a few times, Deon was almost 200 grand in the hole while trying his best to maintain the image of an executive.

Multiply the amount of money he spent himself by a couple of thousand more customers, he knew that the numbers were ridiculous and that at least eighty percent of the generated income of the place, minus expenses, was either being held in a safe or funneled one way or another. His plan was to find out where all that cash was going because the mansion didn't accept checks or credit card unless it was for a wedding. The weddings were held offsite away from where the real business took place. With twenty acres of land separating the main house from the catering hall, there was no way that Mr. Webster's secret could be discovered.

A lot of money was being generated and Deon wanted most of it, in cash. It wasn't the kind of operation that could be extorted, but he was gonna find a way to get his piece of the pie. Putting together a crew was his priority, because he knew he couldn't pull off the job without help. Cindy was the only insider that he had and he wanted to figure out a way to maximize her potential in his plan.

Chapter 19
Devising a Plan

It didn't take long for Deon to figure out that he couldn't conduct business the same way at the mansion as he did with Mr. Brown. The mansion's operation was on a totally different level and even his men would have a hard time comprehending the complexities involved. However, he knew that he was going to at least need Tweak if he stood any chance at all of robbing the place of its wealth. Tweak had been an integral part of his operation from the beginning and Deon didn't want to leave the impression that he was a liar by having Tweak believe that he was close to accomplishing his plan of bringing twenty million dollars to the Hoodfellas as he had been telling them. He decided to approach Tweak individually and asked for a private one-on-one meeting. "Tweak, look, you're one of the brightest men of the crew and I know you might be able to understand my plan on the grander scheme of things than the rest. So I'm just gonna be honest and tell you that we're running low on cash and I need your help to formulate a plan to get this money. The job at the mansion is proving to be harder than I originally thought, but I can't tell the fellas what's been going on because they won't understand." Crazy D was very forthcoming with Tweak and he appreciated Crazy D's honesty. "Never mind the money you spent, let's see how we're gonna get this big money from the mansion," Tweak said. He continued, "I ain't no punk, but I'm also not a killer and from what you've told us about this place, a whole lot of motherfuckers will have to get killed if we want to rob this place." There was uncertainty in Tweak's voice, but Crazy D assured him that he would not be involved in any killing. Crazy D always understood that Tweak's genius mind was his best asset, so he made sure he kept him out of harm's way.

While in prison, Crazy D was cool with a guy name Tom Li who was part of the Chinese mafia and this guy was connected to a few ninjas for hire and these ninjas were like silent exterminators, but they didn't come cheap. Tom Li met Crazy D during an altercation in the yard between the Neo Nazis and the Asian guys. The Neo Nazis outnumbered the Asians three to one when Tom Li found himself cornered and half his men were potentially facing death at the hands of the Neo Nazi crew. Crazy D had a lot of influence in the prison by then and when he took notice of the Neo Nazi charging towards the Asians, he stepped in. It was a beef that could've potentially gotten Crazy D himself in trouble with brothers in the yard, but he acted on instincts, and he didn't like the Neo Nazis.   "This ain't your beef Crazy D. You might as well take your boys and go on about your business," said the Neo Nazi leader whose body was covered with tattoos of swastikas and everything else that represented hate. "Anything that happens in the yard while I'm out here is my business. You might want to tell your clown ass crew to step back before there's bloodshed out here," Crazy D retorted. It was the beginning of a new alliance between Blacks and Asians that hadn't been formed in the prison system since it's existence, but Crazy D managed to do it during this brief altercation. The Asians, Blacks and Hispanics were united for the first time at Walpole even if it was only for a brief month. Li never forgot the favor and he assured Crazy D that he would pull any strings for him if he ever needed a favor.

After initiating contact with Tom Li in prison, Crazy D was able to guarantee himself an army of a dozen ninjas who were would kill at will for a sum of one million dollars. The Chinese mafia, though criminals, were men of their word. A ten percent deposit was agreed upon up front and the rest had to be paid after the job was done. It was a bargain price for the job that Crazy D needed them to do. While the Hoodfellas held down the fort at Brown's enterprise, Tweak and Crazy D started to work on a plan to rob the mansion.

With her salacious mouth, Cindy was able to take still pictures of the vault area and the layouts of the building in the surveillance room while giving the head of security the blowjob of his life. She sucked his dick so well, he went to sleep briefly after busting a nut and she capitalized on it. She was able to use a jump drive to download and copy still photos of each room and secured areas of the mansion. Security posts were the most important because Crazy D wanted to make sure there were no miscalculations. Even with the help of the ninjas, his hired crew, Tweak and Cindy, Crazy D realized that he couldn't pull off the job. He needed more help and the only way to do that was to bring in his law enforcement buddies from the Brown enterprise. High tech was the only way to go and the impossible mission forced Crazy D to steal a page right out of the movie, Mission Impossible.

Chapter 20

Marty and Bob

Marty and Bob were what most people in Boston referred to as "po white trash." It's not that there was so much about them that was trashy, they just didn't have the opportunities that most white people have. Born to a heroin addicted mother and his dad unknown to him, Marty was a very rebellious kid who grew up hating everything about his world. Teased since he was a child for the cheap clothes that his mother often bought him from the Goodwill store and the cheap sneakers from Kmart, Marty had developed some tough skin and the fighting skills to go along with it. With no way out of the South Boston projects, Marty sought to become a boxer at the age of 15. A lanky white kid with the speed of a turtle and the determination of a tiger, Marty was able to beat up a few of his opponents in the ring until he met his match one day, another white boy with more skills and speed than him.

The scheduled five round fight between Marty and the new kid named Bob didn't last more than three rounds. Bob was more skilled in every aspect of the word and seemed more hungry to win than Marty was. Marty was ahead on the scorecards before Bob connected on an uppercut that sent his opponent flying and landing flat on his back on the canvas. The count was up to eight as Marty struggled to get up, but it just wasn't his day. His confidence was shattered and he wanted to know who the new kid was that knocked him out with one punch.

Bob's life was no different from Marty's. He grew up in the Savin Hill section of Dorchester and saw very little of his prostitute mother. Left to fend for himself at a young age, Bob became very self-sufficient. While his mother battled alcoholism, her inability to stay sober prevented her from getting a job. At night, she would wander the streets while Bob was left in the house on his own with his younger brother and sister. With a limited income provided by the welfare department of the state of Massachusetts, Bob's mother could hardly afford to keep food on the table. Working as a drunken prostitute, his mother earned less than minimum wage, and the money she earned on the street was just enough to quench her thirst for alcohol. Bob was ridiculed at school because of his poor hygiene. By the time he was 15 years old, he was always fighting his peers while defending his mother's honor. Most of the children had heard the rumor about his mother being a drunk and a prostitute and they used it to tease Bob. The gym was his sanctuary. It was there he developed the self-esteem needed to survive as a young man.

After the fight, Marty went to look for Bob to congratulate him on a good fight. It was then that they discovered they had so much in common. The two became best friends and sparring partners. All their hopes rode on the fact that they thought they could fight. Unfortunately, those hopes were dashed when they met this young man named Michael Smith from Roxbury in the ring. Marty was the first to fight Michael. The cocky kid from Roxbury knocked Marty out in the first round and broke his jaw. Bob was so pissed he jumped in the ring to go after Michael. And again, the unfortunate happened when Michael connected with a right hook to the weak jaw of Bob and he was knocked out with his buddy, both had broken jaws. It was the last time the two of them had ever gotten in the ring because they now walk around with glass jaws.

Marty and Bob started committing petty crimes and soon found themselves in juvenile detention centers. And later in their lives they became addicted to alcohol and never recovered. They did quite a few stints in prison as adults. Even after they both got sober they were still looking for a big score, and that's how they were brought to the attention of Crazy D.

Chapter 21
Birds of a Feather

Crazy D recruited Marty and Bob to take on the impossible role of officers Steve Flynn and Ray Bratton. Their heights and weight might've been inches apart and a few pounds more or less than the real cops, but it was close enough for Crazy D to work with. The two-knucklehead cops were surprised when they walked into Mr. Brown's building to collect their weekly extortion money to find Crusher and Short Dawg with semi-automatic weapons pointed at the back of their necks. They were tied up and taken to an abandoned building in Roxbury where two security men from the crew and Crusher were watching them. While in the custody of Crusher, molded casts of their faces were taken by this out of work sculptor recruited by Crazy D to create masterpieces that would liken the men to

Bratton and Flynn. The sculptor was more than eager to finally get some work. He was hesitant at first, but fifty grand in cash was convincing enough for him to get involved. However, he made one request and that was to keep his identity hidden from the cops by wearing a ski mask. After the mold was done, the sculptor worked relentlessly to get the faces as close as possible to the likeness of the cops. In fact, they were almost perfect. The two cops were stripped of their clothes, ID's, guns and badges and all the items transformed the two hooligans to police officers at least until the job was done, anyway.

No Neck and three men from the crew kidnapped the two cops on the last day of their workweek before their two days off. Crazy D had a 48-hour window to do what he needed to do; before the two crooked cops were reported missing. The barrel of .45 shotgun made it easy for Bratton to call his wife to tell her that he was going to sleep at the police station for the next couple of days because he was trying to close a case that he had been working on for a while. His wife was used to him not coming home when he had to work long hours. Flynn was single and had no one to report to. Meanwhile, Crazy D made sure that his plan was fool proof and would be executed within that timeframe. Marty and Bob went from delinquents to police officers with a guaranteed payday of one hundred thousand dollars each for a job that would last no more than 48 hours. The two friends couldn't wait to get their assignments and they were looking forward to living it up in Vegas the following weekend.

A necessary crew of over 30 men was recruited for the job and it was time for Crazy D to let everybody in on their roles. Everyone showed up at the meeting at a warehouse in South Boston in a limousine provided by Crazy D. He didn't want to risk anything so he made sure that no one knew where the meeting was going to take place until they were picked up by the driver. A background check was run of every single player to make sure that no one from the crew had a history of snitching. A cleanup crew was also hired. A federal informant could've easily folded Crazy D's plan, so he took every precaution to make sure that didn't happen. Crusher and Short Dawg made sure the place was secure and no one was in the vicinity. Though there's no honor among thieves, Crazy D felt comfortable enough with his crew and he trusted that they would carry out their assignments. The twelve ninjas, Marty and Bob, Tweak, Cindy, and Crazy D all sat around in a circle on crates as Mean T and Short Dawg posted as security in front of the warehouse. No Neck and a few men had to stay back at Mr. Brown's.

Chapter 22

Moving Forward With the Plan

Crazy D strategically planned on robbing the place on Sunday because the mansion made the most money on the weekend and there was less traffic on Sunday evening. Most of the patrons had left except for a few nymphomaniacs and indulgers who decided to stick around for the whole weekend because they couldn't get enough pussy and drugs to satisfy their needs. The mansion was the ultimate haven for the highlife. Everything that a man could possibly dream about was available at the mansion: fine food, fine wine, fine women, pure cocaine, the best liquor and unlimited private entertainment. It should've been called The Pleasure Palace because that's how some of the patrons saw it. Of course, not everyone took part in all of the activities offered at the mansion, but for the most part, all of the men took part in the sex.

The beaming sun was slowly taking shelter behind the mountains as Crazy D and his crew got ready to invade the Webster mansion. By the time dusk settled in, the men were all in black with ski masks over their faces and all kinds of semi-automatic weapons were being placed in strategic areas in case someone had to be shot. There's always that risk when this kind of event is taking place. Silencers, infrared and scopes were attached to the barrel of every gun as Crazy D planned to take over the place quietly. Tweak monitored every part of the mansion from his remote location in a high tech van equipped with every type of multimedia gadget needed to help the crew navigate through the mansion. Cindy had done her duty by placing the hidden cameras in places that gave Tweak a bird's eye view of every corner and every hall. Earpieces were worn by Crazy D and his men and they were able to communicate with Tweak as they made their way throughout the house.

It took Cindy a week to finally place all of the fifty tiny cameras throughout the house. The head of security who fell in love with her head game bought into her wild plan to have sex all over the mansion for a week. It was their little cat-and-mouse game and walk on the wild side as they tried to avoid being caught by Mr. Webster. She even dared him to have sex in Mr. Webster's office while he was out and the idiot agreed. The madam's office was the only significant place left untouched throughout the house. Every hall was monitored, but the two big clowns with the two big guns who stood watch at the vault had two cameras on them. Because it was an underground business, Mr. Webster only reported the legit side of his business to the government. Most of the cash he earned through his prostitution ring was kept in the vault. Cindy was able to find out everything about the business from her security friend because her pussy had his nose wide open. He felt special because she had chosen him to be with and he believed every lie when she told him, "Sugar Bear, You know I'm only still working here to pay off some bills. I wanna be with you and you only." "I know baby. As soon as I leave my wife you can quit this job and we can get married," his stupid ass responded. He completely forgot that she was working as a high priced prostitute and her job was to get men to spend money at the mansion. Oh, the power of the pussy!

Crazy D reprised his role as a customer as he made his way through the front door of the mansion wearing a gray single-breasted, three-button tailor made Italian suit, white shirt, black moccasins and sunglasses. He looked like a bored superstar on a Sunday evening. "Mr. Campbell, as a return customer, you can take advantage of our Sunday special tonight," said the madam. "What is your special?" he asked. "You get two girls for the price of one," said the madam. "No, I'll just stick to my regular girl," he told her. Cindy was called immediately and brought to the main foyer of the mansion to greet Deon. As Deon and Cindy made their way towards the room, he whispered in her ear, "I need you to take care of that fat security bastard." He was referring the to the security guy that Cindy had been fucking at the mansion. After getting to the room Cindy was given an earpiece and small microphone that looked like a diamond piece was placed on a gold chain that Deon supposedly brought as gift for her.

In the meantime, the twelve ninjas made their way through the back woods and climbed over the wall using ropes as Tweak guided them to a clear path as the cameras went clockwise and counterclockwise. The ninjas looked like former Olympic gymnasts as the somersaulted their way above the high wall into the mansion yard. Outfitted in all black, they were hard to spot in the dark. A security guard was placed in a tower that gave him an overview of the property with a big spotlight going back and forth a round the property. That was only momentary as he soon found himself on the floor in the tower after one of the ninjas stuck a knife in his throat. The spotlight was not being monitored by one of the ninjas. Though he continued with the same movement and direction the security guard was following, he allowed the ninjas more time to get from point A to B before he swung the spotlight around.

A sharp poisonous flying star landed between the eyes of one of the armed security guards and he was caught by two ninjas before he could fall on his back. His body was dragged back to the woods as one of the ninjas took his post. It was gonna be a long night because Mr. Webster had a security man guarding every 50 ft of the property and it was a big ass property. The men counted almost 50 armed security guards. The most important location that Crazy D needed access to was the central video room where the head security guard was monitoring every room in the mansion, because it was a Sunday, he worked alone. Mr. Webster figured that traffic was light and there was no need to have additional security. However, Mr. Webster also had a set of monitors in his bedroom that his security didn't know about.

Crazy D had no weapon because he was searched before he was allowed inside the mansion. He had to rely on his bare-knuckle skills in case any trouble came his way. After explaining to Cindy what he needed her to do while in the room with her for about fifteen minutes, he wanted to set his plan in motion. Cindy walked out of the room knowing that the fat security guard was watching her every move. She walked straight to the monitoring room where he was stationed to see him. "What are you doing here? You have a client in the room waiting," said the fat bastard. "That motherfucker is done already. He's not like you, he's one of those one-minute men," she said. "Baby, now you know you ain't never gonna find no man that put it down like me," he said confidently, but inside, she was laughing because Mr. Fat Security's dick was shorter than her pinky finger. She couldn't understand why men with small dicks can't acknowledge that they have a small dick. She didn't want to divert from her plan, so she got on bended knees and unzipped his pants and took all four inches of his dick in her mouth. The plan was to keep him from watching the monitors as Crazy D made his way out of the room to the vault area. The warmth of her sensible mouth comforted the shaft of his penis and he soon found himself drifting into a peaceful and quiet moan as he closed his eyes to take in the kind of heaven that nature intended for men.

"Daddy, I love when you close your eyes while I suck your dick. It's telling me that you enjoy what I'm doing," she said to him, but it was also her cue to inform Crazy D that the coast was clear. He heard it loud and clear through his earpiece as the words were transmitted from the mini microphone dangling from her chain. Cindy hated the security guard with a passion because she found out he was the man who shot her friend. Her first instinct was to take a bite out of his short dick then shove it in his mouth, but she couldn't. She had to follow the plan. As she licked her way around the fat bastard's dick, Crazy D tiptoed to the back of the building toward the vault.

Meanwhile, Tweak was monitoring everything from the van when he came upon the image of Mr. Webster in his room. With the push of a button from a remote control, two fake wall panels came apart and a backdrop of monitors were revealed. Tweak had no idea who the man was, but he assumed it was Mr. Webster because Cindy had labeled each room where she had placed the cameras. The fat security guard thought it would be fun to fuck Cindy in Mr. Webster's room once. "That motherfucker thinks he's the only one who can live like a king, huh? Well, take this Mr. King. Come here, baby," he said to Cindy. She approached him timidly with a naughty look on her face and smiled. Her garter belt, crotchless panties, high heels and bare breasts had his juices flowing as he lay across the California king size bed. Even while lying on his back his gut had to be giggled out of the way so she could get to his dick. She coyly straddled him as she could've easily been reading a newspaper for better entertainment while he half stroked her to boredom. "Take this! You love this dick, don't you?" he said as he humped harder and harder. She was trying her best to keep from yawning, but the acting continued, "Yes daddy, that's it. That's my spot. I'm about to cum," she revealed in her best phony voice. "Don't cum yet, baby. I wanna bust that nut with you," he told her. It took only two more strokes from this fool to fill his condom with semen and they had only been at it for five minutes. It was while he went to the bathroom to take leak that Cindy took out the two tiny cameras from the middle of her hair and set them in the room. And it was a good thing she did that she did plant those cameras because Mr. Webster almost caught an image of Crazy D sneaking down the hall to the vault. "Stay put. Find a place to hide, quick," he whispered through the transmitter to Crazy D. "I just saw a man watching a bunch of monitors in his room and one of the cameras might be set up in your area. I need to zoom in to see what he's looking at before you make your next move," Tweak warned.

Tweak zoomed in on Mr. Webster with the cameras and that's when he noticed the monitors were set up to watch the hall that led to the vault and another placed directly on the vault. While Crazy D was caught between a rock and a hard place, the ninjas continued to follow through with their plans. At least ten security guards had been taken out and one got his head chopped off as he was about to reveal that there were some intruders on the premises. The shard blade of the saw went from the back of his neck and almost disappeared as his head fell to the ground and blood gushed from his body. Entering the building would prove more of a task as the Ninjas faced the fiercest men in the mansion. The huge columns provided a shield for the first four Ninjas who orchestrated their move to take out four security guards in unison. The roundhouse kicks landed directly to the security guards' head and knives planted in their throats as the ninjas charged towards the mansion. No one could utter a word as the ninjas moved with the speed of light to conquer these big men whose machine guns were rendered useless because the element of surprise was too strong for them.

Mr. Webster was fixated on the monitors because he convinced himself that he had seen the shadow of a person through one of the monitors. "Kevin, can you send somebody to check hallway five. I think I saw some," Mr. Webster instructed the fat bastard whose dick was now limped because Cindy made sure he busted a nut while Crazy D snuck out of the room. He quickly zipped up his pants and refocused back on the monitors. "Ten-four," he responded to confirm that he had received

Mr. Webster's orders. The fat bastard's name was Kevin, but he looked more like a Bubba. He called into his radio for two men to go check hallway # 5. Two mean looking 6ft-7 giants armed with Tech-9 Uzis headed down to hall five watching their steps carefully. The mansion was so big Mr. Webster decided to designate numbers to the hallways to make it easier for his staff. As the two security guards got closer to the hallway, they decided to split so they could cover both ends of the hallway. By then, Crazy D had decided to climb over a large beam that spread across the hallway's ceiling to help secure the structure of that part of the building. One of the security guards was too busy looking for someone on the ground. He didn't notice it when Crazy D wrapped the sleeves of his jacket around his big ass neck allowing him no room to breathe as Crazy D jumped down from one side of the beam. While the weight of Crazy D's body pulled on the jacket around the tall security guard's neck bringing his body toward the ground, the security guard's head ascended toward the beam leaving his feet dangling, causing him to suffocate until he lost the air supply to his brain.

Crazy D shielded himself behind the massive man as he played ventriloquist with the dead body to the security guard on the other end of the hallway while losing strength from holding up the weight of the massive man. He gave the guy a signal that everything was okay as he lifted the right hand of the dead security before dragging the body out of the way. He quickly took the guard's gun and dashed towards the other guard while hiding behind the columns between the hallway. By then it was no use because Mr. Webster had witnessed all the action and a call went out to the security force of the premise. However, before he could press the button to warn the police department about the security

breach at the mansion, Crazy D quickly called
Tweak on the two-way transmitter radio to inform
him to cut off the electrical power from the pole
outside and to have the two delinquents posing as
officers Bratton and Flynn to respond to the
incident. Mr. Webster thought he pressed the button
just in time.

The white boys, Marty and Bob, showed up at
the gate with their guns drawn. "We received a call
that there were some problems here. Their faces
were all too familiar at the mansion because they
also had their hands in Mr. Webster's business as
lookouts and inside informants. They had been on
payroll for many years. Soon after the security gate
opened, the two security guards found themselves
handcuffed to each other butt naked with a big post
between them. The two delinquents were also
clowns. It was just the kind of action they were
looking for. Officer Bratton's and Flynn's guns were

now in the hands of two crazy clowns who didn't know what to do with themselves, but they had set their own rules prior to taking the job. "We're not killers, we're gonna let these motherfuckers kill each other if they want to, but we're not shooting anybody," Bob said to Marty. "Hell nah we're not shooting anybody. We're in this for the money and that's it," Marty replied. "I just want to make sure we're both on the same page," Bob confirmed.

Meanwhile, ten more security guards swarmed toward the vault and an additional five went to secure Mr. Webster and the madam's safety. Mr. Webster took out his nickel-plated .45 as he and the madam were directed toward a safe room in the basement of the house by security. "If I come out of this alive, every single one of you will be rich for the rest of your lives," Mr. Webster told his security men. Darkness took over the mansion and the Ninja's were navigating throughout the building with flashlights, something that was part of their plan from the very beginning. Different signals were being sent by the light beams and the security force didn't know what to do as the ninjas continued to get to them before they could react. Some of the soft ones gave up and were tied up in a room together while the rest of them continued to fight. Gunfire erupted throughout the building as everyone was running for cover.

The four Russian guards guarding the vault had sworn off their lives to keep anybody from penetrating that vault. Their families were set up by Mr. Webster and they owed him their lives. They formed a circle around the vault as the waited for the surge to happen. By then, the Hoodfellas had called on their goons to swarm the mansion and take it over. A team of twenty men dressed in army fatigue showed up at the mansion with grenades, dynamite and other bombs waiting for the order to

blow up the place. The TNT was being set up
around the building by the men and Tweak was
nervous while waiting in the van outside for the real
cops to show up. All the patrons and call girls were
gathered, blindfolded, tied up and led to the catering
hall where they would witness the demise of the
best pussy haven they had ever known. Most of
them were naked and some of the kinkiest ones
were still in cuffs with leather straps and other
dominatrix and submissive apparel on.

Short Dawg wore his ski mask the whole time
as he was instructed to while making sure
everything went accordingly as far as the safety of
the patrons. He was also ordered to make an
example of anybody who resisted. As the group of
patrons was being led to the catering hall, one state
senator declared, "I'm a senator. I will have your
life if you force me to walk out there, tied up in the
woods with no clothes. That's kidnapping." "You'll

be napping alright if you don't shut the fuck up. I'll knock your ass out and you'll be taking a long nap," said Short Dawg. "I'm not going anywhere with you and neither are they," said the senator. As Short Dawg's crew moved the people in a single file, the line came to an abrupt stop because of the senator. Without as much as saying a word, Short Dawg punched the senator in the face, took his left leg and broke it in half. "Now you better hop your ass up to the woods before I shoot your other leg," said Short Dawg. The senator said nothing and hopped fast with a sudden sense of urgency toward the catering hall 20 acres away along with the rest of the group.

Crusher and a crew of ten men stayed back at Mr. Brown's and were given specific instructions as to what action should be taken at 11:00 pm. As the group of ninjas spread around the compound to make sure that every security guard in sight was accounted for or at least subdued, Crazy D started taking out as many security guards as possible that crossed his path. Armed with a machine gun and the desire to get to his prize, he had no mercy on any fools who thought they had a chance to stop him. One of the five Russian men in the vault room didn't even see the twelve-inch knife entering his nuts with the force stronger than a jack hammer. Crazy D snuck up behind the man using a quarter as a distraction. He rolled the quarter toward the vault and the man reacted with his gun, but by the time he stopped firing shots, his nuts were on the ground in a pile of blood next to his body. The square vault was so big that the guards had decided to cover one side each. In the darkness while of their comrades screamed in pain, the other three Russian men fired their guns in his direction taking out whatever life he had left in him.

Through the barrage of bullets, Crazy D managed to blow off the head of another of the

Russian men leaving him two guys to deal with. Now they could only use two sides of the square vault to shield themselves from harm. While still in total darkness, the two men walked around talking to each other in Russian to avoid shooting each other by accident. Meanwhile, Crazy D used the recorder on his cell phone to record one of the men. As they walked around in circle, silence fell for a quick second and Crazy D used the recorded voice to lure one of the men towards him. As he approached, he damn near unloaded his automatic weapon on the man. The other guy called out for his comrade, but only Crazy D's voice answered from the other side of the vault, "I think your boy's dead. You're the only one left." Crazy D's voice echoed around the room and the man was trying to figure out which side of the steel vault the voice was coming from. "I'm gonna kill you. Fucking bastard!" the man screamed in a thick Russian accent then continued, "You're a man and I'm a man. We should settle this like men.". Crazy D whispered to Tweak to turn the power back on. Now the man could see his friends' bodies lying in a pool of blood in plain site. He was angered by the events. "Come on you bastard. Come get a piece of me if you have the balls!" he screamed after throwing down his gun. His huge 7ft muscular frame was intimidating, but he was confident that he could take out Crazy D even without seeing him. Crazy D appeared to see a blood-thirsty man standing with his arm out and enough anger in his eyes to blow up a whole city. "I'm from the hood and this is how we do it in the hood," Crazy D said as he emptied his clip on the huge man who charged towards him through the barrage of bullets. Before the man could fall to the ground, his hands had reached Crazy D's neck and Crazy D wasn't sure if the life was about to be choked out of him until he noticed the man's knees buckled and his huge body hit the cement floor.

Getting to the vault was one thing, but opening the vault was going to be an impossible task. The only person with the combination to the vault was Mr. Webster and his security men had taken him downstairs through a tunnel that led to the catering hall 20 acres away. Kevin, the fat bastard with the infatuation for Cindy, stayed in the monitoring room the whole time claiming he was gonna protect her. Cindy played along as she waited for her opportunity. "Baby, I'm scared. These people might try to kill me. I need a gun to protect myself," she told Kevin. "I ain't really supposed to give you no gun, but in a situation like this, why not," he said to her as he handed her a loaded .9-Millimeter with an extra clip. The commotion was getting closer and closer to them and Kevin started to panic. "Are we gonna be safe here?" Cindy asked. "I know an even safer place. Follow me," he told her.

Kevin led the way with his gun drawn as he found the route to the catering hall in the basement. Cindy was following him close as she contemplated unloading a couple of rounds into the back of his head. Mr. Webster, the madam and his men were at least three quarters of the way ahead of them, but the fat bastard was trying his best to catch up to them, as his breathing grew louder and shorter with fear. His intimidating size was the only thing scary about Kevin. He had no heart. While trying to run to safety, there was one crazy motherfucker in full pursuit. Crazy D was determined to find Mr. Webster so he could open the vault. He radioed for the Marty and Bob to stand at the front gate in case real popo showed up.

By this time, Tweak was back to monitoring the mansion again. He noticed that Kevin went down a flight of stairs and disappeared into oblivion. He relayed the message to Crazy D via radio and Crazy D followed behind them. Those stairs led directly down to the tunnel. As sweat poured down the brows of Crazy D, he took off his shirt leaving on a wife-beater that exposed his defined muscle toned body while carrying an AK-47 in one hand and an Uzi in the other. He was like Rambo running down the tunnel to find Mr. Webster. Crazy D had come too far to allow the prize to elude him. He needed to pay people and deliver on his promise to his crew. The Asian connection was in a room waiting for their final payment as well. Crazy D had too much riding on it, so he had to find a way.

When Mr. Webster and his men made it to the catering hall they were very careless and a little too loud as they thought they were the only ones in the building. Short Dawg could hear the commotion, so he took his position with his men behind a couple of doors before shutting off the lights. As the group entered the catering hall from the basement, Webster was sweating out of his pores and the madam's make-up was running like Tammy Faye Baker. Short Dawg signaled to the patrons to keep quiet by raising his gun and placing a finger over his mouth. Just when the group finally thought they were safe after entering the room and turning on the lights, Short Dawg and his men had their weapons pointed directly at them and ordered everyone to drop their weapon. The guns were collected and Mr. Webster and his group were ordered to take a seat on the floor on the opposite side of the room across from the patrons. The senator was still screaming from the pain of his broken leg, but Short Dawg threatened to break the other one as well if he didn't shut the hell up.

Mr. Webster's attire set him apart from the rest of his men. The Rolex watch, the Italian shoes and tailor made attire made him look more distinguished than all the men in black suits who surrounded him. Short Dawg alerted Crazy D right away over the radio, "I think I mighta caught myself a big fish. He looks like the man you might need to talk to." "Where are you right now?" I'm in the catering hall with the hostages, I mean customers," said Short Dawg. "Don't do anything until I get there," Crazy D ordered.

Short Dawg saw the diamond sparkling on the presidential Rolex around Mr. Webster's wrist and thought to himself, *Crazy D don't have to know about this Rolex.* He went over and ordered Mr. Webster to take off the expensive watch. "I think it looks better on my arm, what do you think?" he asked the group. Everyone shook their heads in agreement. Mr. Webster gave him a killer look as if to say "you're gonna pay for this with your life." Short Dawg wanted to wipe that mean look off his face right away, but he chilled because Crazy D had ordered him to. "I ain't much into bling, but this is the kind of bling I can rock," said Short Dawg as he walked away with the watch on his wrist.

Short Dawg and his men weren't paying attention when Kevin and Cindy made their way through the door. Kevin, still shaken from all the commotion, walked through the door with his gun in hand and ordered Short Dawg to put down his weapon. It was more like a stand-off because Short Dawg would not back down. Cindy had seen enough. She drew her gun on Kevin and ordered him to put down his gun. This situation became a little confusing because Short Dawg had no idea who Cindy was and she had no idea who Short Dawg was. While the three of them were trying to figure who was whom, Crazy D had made it through the door. While the stand-off continued, the madam reached into her garter belt and pulled out her nickel plated .25 that she kept hidden under her dress. As she aimed for Cindy's head Crazy D shot her dead between the eyes as he pushed Cindy out of harm's way. Kevin's finger hit the trigger while aiming for Short Dawg, but Cindy's bullet pierced his heart from behind before he could press the trigger all the way. Kevin fell on his face, but with tears in his eyes, Cindy turned him over and shot him once more after reminding him that he had killed her best friend.

The room was quiet, as the patrons didn't know their fate. There were so many guns in the room and so many bullets flying, everybody was scared. Crazy D was fixated on the distinguished looking man. "You must be Webster," he said pointing to the man. "Who might you be?" Mr. Webster said sarcastically. "Your worst nightmare," Crazy D answered. "Do I know you from somewhere?" Mr. Webster asked. "No, but you will in a few minutes," Crazy D said as he ordered Mr. Webster to get up from the floor. "You and I are going for a walk because we have business to discuss. "Do you want me to come along?" Cindy asked. "No. Why don't you stay here and get to know Short Dawg better. Help him and the crew clean up the place," Crazy D said. Two men from the crew grabbed each of Mr. Webster's arms as they walk back through the tunnel to the mansion. "I can make you a rich man," Mr. Webster told Crazy D. "How can you make a rich man rich?" Crazy D asked. "I'm worth more money than Donald Trump. If we can work something out, it can be all yours," Mr. Webster said to Crazy D. "What are we going to work out?" asked Crazy D. "I know what you are after, but you can't get to it without me, so you might as well make a deal with me," he said firmly. "We're gonna deal alright," Crazy D whispered under his breath as he took his final step into the room where the vault was located.

Crazy D already knew that his time in the city was limited. Mr. Webster's negotiating skills would be put to the test, but he had ground to stand on. "I can die a happy man today because I've lived a great life. I've been rich since I was a teenager and I have fucked more women than most NBA players or any celebrity in America. You can just shoot me now because you'll never get the combination to the safe," he told Crazy D. "You see, this is your first problem; you talk too goddamn much," Crazy told Mr. Webster. He ordered one of the men to grab a chair that was nearby. Mr. Webster took a quick overview of his men lying on the floor in the pool of blood and decided to accept his fate, but only if it was gonna be that easy.

After sitting Mr. Webster in the chair with his hands and feet tied behind him, Crazy D left him in the room with two of his armed men only to return with a sewing kit. One of the men held his head in place while Crazy pulled out his needle, thread, and sewed Mr. Webster's mouth shut. "Now, here's how we're gonna negotiate; I do all the talking while you nod your head in agreement. Basically, you're gonna agree to my plan or further negotiation tactics will be used because I'm not interested in killing you," Crazy D revealed. As blood ran down his lips from the stitches, Mr. Webster continued to act like he was the Teflon Don. "We can do this the easy way or we can do it the hard way, what's it gonna be, the easy way?" Crazy D asked. Mr. Webster didn't nod his head in agreement. "I guess we're gonna have to do this the hard way," Crazy D said as he pulled out a pair of commercial electrical wire cutters from his back pocket. "Take his shoes off," he ordered one of his men. After taking off Mr. Webster's shoes and socks, Crazy D too the wire cutter and slowly cut the small toe off Mr. Webster's right foot. Mr. Webster didn't say a word as he withstood the pain. Crazy D ordered his men to cut off every single toe before leaving the room.

One of the men was all too eager to take part in the sinister act. When Crazy D came back, he found all of Mr. Webster's ten toes on the floor, blood all over the place and sweat pouring from Mr. Webster's brow. Mr. Webster was shaken at the site of Crazy D now, because he had no idea what Crazy D had up his sleeve next. "I think he's ready to tell us the combination to the safe, is that right?" Mr. Webster nodded his head to agree. "I'll go through the numbers and you just nod when I get to the right one. As Crazy D counted from one to ten Mr. Webster stopped him at each correct number while giving him the combination to the vault. Crazy D couldn't believe his eyes after opening the vault. There had to be at least 200 million dollars in cash and an additional 20 million in jewelry. "Tweak, send the boys in here with the bags and tell them to hurry up cause we don't have much time left," Crazy D said through his mic. Within minutes a crew of twenty men showed up with big bags and a truck to carry all the money out. Before leaving, Crazy D handed two bags filled with cash to the leader of the Asian connection. While looking through the bag, the man smiled because he knew there was at least five million dollars in those bags.

Crazy D needed to make sure no stone was left unturned. He called for Marty and Bob to meet him in the vault room as he sat two of the dead Russian men against the wall. While the camera was rolling, he asked Bob and Marty to shoot the two dead men in the back of the head execution style while smiling into the camera. Bob and Marty hesitated at first, but after confirming that the two men were already dead, they went ballistic as they unloaded bullets into the men like wild cowboys. It was all caught on camera while they were still wearing the faces and clothes of officers Flynn and Bratton and using the cops' guns for the act. Bob and Marty was told they'd be earning a quarter of a million dollars for their efforts. After they left the room, the two white boys changed back into their own clothing, peeled the masks off their faces before getting behind the wheel of the Mayback to drive Crazy D to his next destination. There was no need for Marty and Bob to go to the final meeting because their services were almost complete.

Crazy D had completely forgotten about Mr. Webster who almost passed out from the pain as well as his money being taken before his eyes. "Boss, what do you want us to do with him?" one of the men asked. "Go wait in the truck. I got it," he told them. Crazy D walked back to the vault one last time to finally take care of something he had wanted to do since he came out of jail. "Mr. Webster, or should I call you Wally? I think it's time we get a little better acquainted," he said. He pulled out a picture of his mother, "Do you remember this woman?" It was a picture of Serena when she was young and beautiful and he was sure that it would bring back some memories for Wally. Wally could barely keep his eyes open, but he recognized the woman in the picture. "Well, that's how beautiful she was. This was her after you beat the crap out of her," Crazy D said after pulling out another picture the police took of his mother while she was in the hospital. Anger started to set in and Crazy D was about to live up to the nickname he's carried all of his life. Fear gripped the heart of Mr. Webster and he was just hoping that Crazy D would shoot him already. "She was a defenseless woman and you beat her until she was incapacitated. "I think it's time you learn your fate and you deserve a worse one than my mother, wouldn't you agree?" Mr. Webster's eyes almost fell out their sockets as his face grew with curiosity wondering what painful procedure he was about to undergo at the hands of Crazy D. There was silence for a minute as Crazy turned his back to face the wall.

When Crazy D finally turned back around, he had this sinister look on his face and a satisfied grin as he pulled out a sharp switchblade and stuck it in each of Mr. Webster's thighs before cutting off his dick and left him to die in the vault. He shut the door to the vault as no one knew the combination and the extra thick steel walls of the vault would not release a sound or be penetrated. He wanted Mr. Webster to die in his own pool of blood with his severed dick on his lap.

Crazy D ran back outside to his Mayback where Marty was behind the wheel and Bob in the backseat being driven around like two businessmen.

Short Dawg was instructed to walk out of the building with his men leaving the patrons to think that they were still there monitoring them. "I'm about to turn on the television and I don't wanna hear a word from any of you. The first person who says anything will get a bullet between their eyes," peep warned before turning the television to the news. "I like to watch my news in peace," he continued. Meanwhile, he signaled for his men to start walking out of the building. The television was only turned on to keep the patrons from hearing the men walk out of the building.

Crusher and a few men were instructed to bind Mr. Brown to a chair in the basement, gag him, and to make sure the doors and windows were secured. The final meeting was scheduled to take place at the warehouse with Crazy D his crew before embarking on a final destination. Crazy D had two of his men return the personal belongings of the two cops, including their guns less any bullets. The cops were dressed in their old clothes, their badges and guns were returned to them and they were handcuffed by No Neck and two armed security men from the crew. They were driven to a remote location about an hour away from the city. They would have to walk at least sixty miles of dirt roads and cornfields before finding any sign of civilization. It gave Crazy D and his crew plenty of time to make their getaway.

While the crew waited at the warehouse, Crazy D had Marty and Bob drive him to Mr. Brown's facility because he had one more score to settle. Tremaine Brown knew that he had done dirt in his life, but he had no idea that he had done things that would warrant his death. He kept staring at Crazy D wondering what it is that brought him to his current situation. Perhaps Crazy D was just a nut; he tried to reason. As a hustler, Tremaine Brown could not recount the people he had crossed and their reasons for vengeance against him and Crazy D looked like he was out for more than revenge. He was trying to settle a score. Mr. Brown's heart was beating a mile a minute as he awaited his fate. There was no talking his way out of the situation because the determined look on Crazy D's face was enough for him to recognize that he needed to keep his mouth shut.

Brown had a perturbed look on his face as Crazy D circled around him with a .9- Millimeter revolver in hand. His life could end at any minute, he thought. However, with his hands and feet tied, his soft heart couldn't even make a last ditch effort to fight back. Crazy D was a lot more calculated than Brown gave him credit for. "I'm sure you have no idea who I am and why I'm about to take your life, but I can tell you this, you were a nightmare to someone that was dear to me," Crazy D said with anger in his voice. The confirmation of his death was certain, but he wanted to know why he was dying. "What the hell are you talking about, who are you, really?" Tre asked with his voice cracked. "It doesn't really matter who I am, but I want you to remember this name in your last hour on earth," Crazy D's voice was becoming more sinister with each phrase. Mr. Brown suddenly developed a lump in his throat as he fought for air. "The name Serena Bender is the last thing I want you to remember before you die," Crazy D said as he pulled out his blade and started cutting open Mr. Brown's pants slowly down to his underwear. "You like to watch women prostitute themselves, huh?" Crazy D asked sarcastically. The sharp blade was inches from Mr. Brown's penis as Crazy D started talking to him in a menacing way. Mr. Brown felt his castration was near, so he said nothing back to Crazy D as he anticipated the blade cutting through his flesh on his most private part. His legs started shaking and his eyes were bulging as sweat overtook his face. "Give me one reason to allow you to live. "What have you done for mankind and your community?" Crazy D asked. Mr. Brown couldn't think quickly enough about what he had done for mankind. "I never had a chance in this life because of people like you who like to take advantage of people. Well, your day has come and my mother should've been the last person you hurt!" Crazy D said as he cut into Mr. Brown's penis and castrated him with one flick of the knife. He left him tied up in the chair in the basement so the clean up crew could take care of him.

Marty and Bob met with Short Dawg down on Massachusetts Avenue where Crazy D hopped in the van and gave the keys and title to the brand new Mayback to Bob and Marty. The two crazy white boys couldn't believe Crazy D's generosity and their loyalty was appreciated as Crazy D threw another bag filled with money at them before the van peeled off. Those white boys would take the events that happened to their grave because they would never have to work again. Crazy D changed their lives forever and they knew they didn't stand a chance of becoming anything had they not met Crazy D. Marty and Bob were no different because they were white. They were still from the projects, a white project, and their chances of making it out of the projects was just as slim as any other projects in any ghettos of America. They played the hands that they were dealt and came out on top.

Chapter 23
The Cleanup Crew

Before leaving the mansion, Crazy D gave his men specific instructions to implode the place. Imploding the place would guarantee that Mr. Webster's body wouldn't be found in time for him to be saved. Crazy D wanted him to die a slow and painful death. He also knew that it would take a miracle for the fire department to get the vault open. Webster's fate was pretty much determined. Crazy had accomplished his mission and he had found enough money to last him and his crew a lifetime. There would be no more worries about money and life would be smooth from then on.

The cleanup crew made sure the dynamite was already set in place and everyone except Mr. Webster and the dead bodies were evacuated from the building. It was a shame to see such a beautiful construction get destroyed, but all traces of what took place had to disappear. With the push of a button, all that remained of the mansion was dust and construction debris. Mr. Webster's dream had gone down with him because karma came back to bite him in the ass. All the people he had ever hurt while climbing his way to the top were the reason why a person like Crazy D was thrust into his life.

After blowing up the mansion, the clean up crew made a smooth getaway and they could see the fire trucks and the police lights and sirens headed to the scene as they drove straight to Mr. Brown's facility. Crusher and No Neck had closed down shop before he left and made sure no one was left inside except for Mr. Brown. The place was doused with gasoline inside and out. The crew had no idea that Mr. Brown was in the basement as they poured gasoline throughout the house. After the men walked out, a lighter was flicked on and thrown in the house where a huge fire ensued. Mr. Brown had very little chance to survive as the house was engulfed in flames. The men walked nonchalantly back to the van while the house burned to a crisp. The cleanup crew did their job and it was time for them to collect their share of the prize money. Twenty million dollars was pretty tempting and Crazy D knew better, so he decided to have a drop-off for the money to pay the clean-up crew. Something about the crew was a little too fierce for Crazy D. He took every precaution to make sure there wouldn't be a hit.

Short Dawg and No Neck met with the cleanup crew. They dropped off the agreed million dollars for the job at a vacant lot in Dorchester. No Neck remained behind the wheel of the van while Short Dawg walked half the distance to meet the dude with the bags of money. "We appreciate you looking out for us," said Short Dawg's boy who was in charge of the crew. It was the dude he trusted the most from the cleanup crew, because they had known each other since they were kids. "It's no big deal, I just wanted to make sure y'all got to eat a little," Short Dawg said to him. "Well, I'm a little more hungry than you think, and I'm sorry I have to do this," the man said. Short Dawg reached for his gun as he tried to dash back into the van. Crazy D had told Short Dawg to deal with the cleanup crew exclusively. Unexpectedly, the cleanup crew came out blazing with guns shooting at everything in sight. They thought rest of the money was in the van along with Crazy D. No Neck was able to call Crazy D on his cell phone to report the attack. "We just got ambushed by these cats!" No Neck screamed through the phone before a bullet hit him in the chest. But it was too late for Crazy D to do anything about it as Short Dawg's body was filled with holes from the hail of bullets sprayed by the cleaning crew by the time he jumped back in the van. No Neck caught a couple shots to the head as he tried to ram the van into the men shooting at the van. The men unloaded their automatic weapons and sprayed the van until there was no possibility of any life left in the van. Unfortunately, they didn't find what they'd hoped for. The cleanup crew knew that the job was worth a lot more than the million dollars they were promised. They decided to make it a winner takes-all situation. They should've never bet against Crazy D.

Short Dawg and Crazy D saw their last day on earth that day because of betrayal. All that they had worked for since leaving prison led to their day in hell at the hand of a trusted friend because of the mighty dollar.

Chapter 24

The Getaway

The helicopters hovered above as Crazy D contemplated his next move. He had lost one of his best friends. The cleanup crew was supposed to be Short Dawg's boys. He had grown up with them. He trusted them. He recommended them for the job because he wanted them to eat a little too, but they got greedy and now an all out war had to take place. The only thing that kept Crazy D and the rest of the crew from making a clean getaway was his conflicted conscience. He thought about his days in prison with Short Dawg, how they had become friends and all that they had gone through together. He had never had a friend like Short Dawg who was so loyal. He couldn't let his best friend die in vain. Something had to be done. He also thought about No Neck and all that they had been through in prison together. He wanted to stay true to the game, but he wasn't sure if he should risk it all to avenge his best friend's death. Dishonor was something that Crazy D loathed with a passion and he wanted every single one of those men to pay.

He called Short Dawg's phone again. There was no answer. At least he felt it was his duty to secure the body and give his friend a proper burial. The crew looked on as Crazy tried to decide his next move. They had over 190 million dollars in cash and a 50-room mansion in the hills of Haiti where luxury awaited them. Jean Paul, the Haitian connect that Crazy D met while he was locked up in prison had already secured the mansion for Crazy D and his crew. There was a full staff there to take care of the crew's every need. The Dominican and Haitian chicks waiting to serve his crew were the finest women Jean Paul recruited. Jean Paul himself was a kingpin who got sent to prison on a murder charge. The feds had nothing on him because most of his loot was sent back home to Haiti where he built himself a castle. After he was deported back home, he and Crazy D kept in touch through letters. Jean Paul wanted Crazy D to come down to Haiti to get a taste of the good life because Crazy D had looked out for him in prison.

With no allies in prison, Jean Paul found himself in a bind after beating up a gang member in the shower one day. The gang showed up ready to take him out as the water ran down his body. He looked around and saw no way out as the gang members surrounded him. However, Crazy D found out through the grapevine that Jean Paul was sent to prison after he took out a man who shot his cousin who worked for Jean Paul. His cousin and Jean Paul were partners in the game. Crazy D decided to come to Jean Paul's rescue because of the relationship he shared with his cousin prior to coming to prison.

No punches were ever thrown as Crazy D and his crew showed up and told the gang that hurting Jean Paul was not an option. From then on, the two became friends and Jean Paul vowed to take care of Crazy D and his crew if they ever made it outta prison. Like most dudes on the inside, Jean Paul started telling Crazy D and his crew about his castle in Haiti, but no one believed him. Even after Crazy D came out of jail, he didn't reach out to Jean Paul because he thought Jean Paul was full of shit. It wasn't until Jean Paul started sending him pictures of the castle, his Range Rover, Lexus 470, Mercedes Benz and his women that he started to believe that Jean Paul was the baller that he was claiming to be.

Jean Paul had made over fifty million dollars in the drug game before he was sent to a state prison, but unlike most drug dealers, he was building a foundation back in his home land of Haiti. Jean Paul wasn't flashy and most of his money was sent home because he knew the feds would come knocking one day. Unfortunately, his boy Diggy got caught up with some dude and he was murdered. Jean Paul was a loyal friend, so he decided to take out the whole crew who killed his boy. Diggy was the only family member who sent money to Crazy D's commissary in prison, so Crazy D owed it to him to watch out for Jean Paul while he was locked up.

Crazy D had no idea how he was gonna move all the money that he had out of the country. He started talking to Jean Paul and that's how the getaway plan was formulated. Jean Paul arranged for two helicopters to pick up Crazy D and his crew with the money and then they would be taken to a major cruise ship that Jean Paul had a personal relationship with the captain. He had been doing business with this man for many years on the side. And this captain had earned the trust of custom agents around the world. Jean Paul also had a few custom agents on his payroll in Haiti because most of his business came from Miami. The money would be kept in an isolated room that only the captain had access to and the authorities had never bothered to search that room during his tenure as a captain. Jean Paul would pick up the crew in Labadie, Haiti when they docked there for the tourists to get a view of the impoverished nation.

Jean Paul found it hard to believe that Labadie is part of Haiti when first went there. The United States government has a fifty-year lease on that part of the island. It is kept so clean that it looks like it's a different nation by itself.

The crew wasn't as thick as it once was. Tweak, Crusher and Cindy were all that remained. The hired guns weren't part of the crew. They were hired to do specific jobs and were paid handsomely, but they were loyal to Crazy D. However, one kid in particular stood out to Crazy D and the only way to save that kid was for Crazy D to take him and make him part of the crew. He wasn't gun shy and he had the heart of a lion. He was the kid who smoked most of Mr. Brown's crew and enjoyed every minute of it. His name was Smitty. He would go along to become Crazy D's protégé.

All the money in the world couldn't put Crazy D's mind at ease because he had lost two of his closest friends. He had planned to live it up with them. He was looking forward to having a real family, but that would never be. As the pilots of the helicopters called for the crew to start loading up for departure, Crazy D made a phone call to one of the trusted members of the hired crew. He took a bag of money and handed it to the driver of the van with a few directions to follow. No one knew what was said, Crazy D boarded that helicopter feeling that

Short Dawg and No Neck's death would avenged even if he had to come back himself to do it.

The mood was somber as the crew boarded the ship to head to their destination in Haiti, where a new culture and language awaited them. Only God knows what else, because Jean Paul never led a straight life and no amount of money could lead him to a straight life because the thrill of illegal mischief was what he lived for. Crazy D and his crew may have had all the money in the world, but navigating through Haitian society will prove to be more than a challenge for them.

Before leaving the country, Tweak was able to mail a copy of a tape to the police precinct where Bratton and Flynn worked. On that tape was all the evidence that the state of Massachusetts and the federal government needed to indict the two cops for criminal behavior.

Chapter 25
Reflections

After boarding the ship, Crazy D knelt down in his cabin and closed his eyes as he began to pray, "Lord, I never thought that I would come out of jail to be involved in crimes of this magnitude. I wanted a simple life just like any other man, but society wouldn't let me have that. I didn't earn the right to a second chance, according to society. I had an endless debt to pay because I burned my bridges as a teenager and society has not allowed me to live it down. Lord, I pray that you understand my plight and the reasons I had to do what I've done. To be in this world with nothing means you ain't shit. Sorry Lord, for cussing but ain't no other way to put it. Sometimes I feel the right to be a normal human being was taken from me since birth because of everything that was stacked against me. Only a few of us make it out alive from the projects and Lord, sometimes, I wonder if you answer the prayers from people in the projects.

As I look around me, I see nothing but crackheads, prostitutes, pimps, drug dealers, destitute people and every other bad element that you can think of in these projects. Lord, why do you allow such grief and pain to be concentrated in one area? Are we not chosen from birth like other folk? Did my mother deserve the kind of life that she led? Are we paying for all the pain that my father may have caused others? I was taught that you're a forgiving God, but it doesn't seem like anything has been forgiven in my life. I try as much as I can to pray silently and I know that you know what's going on in my head and my heart. I never meant to kill anybody, Lord, but I live in a world where I have to kill or be killed. My government uses the same motto. They use violence to get ahead and I have had to learn to do the same. I'm one of the little guys trying to get a small piece of the pie. Those who steal and cause others to die are hardly punished on Wall Street, Lord, so why are we punished so harshly in the projects?

I hope you understand that I couldn't go back to living like a savage in a place where most people fight and die everyday for no reason, without gaining anything for it. I wasn't gonna allow the projects to suck me in again, so I decided to fight. I wanted to die for something more and in the process I have taken a few lives. For most people it's a daily struggle to just leave the projects, but I made it, Lord. I'm out now. Lord, I pray that one day you can bless all the projects around the world and offer hope and dreams to young boys and girls like me whose future seems to be destined behind bars, living in a cage like a captured animal. I never wanted anything for free, but no one was willing to give me a chance so I was forced to take it, just like they were forced to take it from somebody else.

Did you purposely create the world this way, Lord? Is it always gonna be survival of the fittest? If it is, I plan to survive from now on because nobody is ever gonna take away my freedom and basic right as a human being ever again.

Why did you have to take Short Dawg and No Neck, Lord? I want to say that I'm sorry, Lord, for all that I have done and I await my fate with strength and dignity because I know that I have sinned and only you can choose the method of your forgiveness. Please bless my new family, the Hoodfellas. Thank you Lord."

A NOVEL FROM THE BESTSELLING AUTHOR OF "MEETING MISS RIGHT" AND "SEXUAL EXPLOITS OF A NYMPHO"

REVISED EDITION

Neglected
SOULS

"Dark alleys, cold and lonely nights just trying to survive... Who can you run to? Neglected Souls made me gasp and grip my heart."
Keshamba Williams, Best Selling Author of Driven and At The Court's Mercy

RICHARD JEANTY

NEGLECTED SOULS

Motherhood and the trials of loving too hard and not enough frame this story...The realism of these characters will bring tears to your spirit as you discover the hero in the villain you never saw coming...

Neglected Souls is a gritty, honest and heart-stirring story of hope and personal triumph set in the ghettos of Boston.

In Stores!!!

A NOVEL FROM THE BESTSELLING AUTHOR THAT BROUGHT YOU "*NEGLECTED SOULS*"

Neglected

NOMORE

THE SEQUEL TO *NEGLECTED SOULS*

RICHARD JEANTY

Jimmy and Nina continue to feel a void in their lives because they haven't a clue about their genealogical make-up. Jimmy falls victims to a life threatening illness and only the right organ donor can save his life. Will the donor be the bridge to reconnect Jimmy and Nina to their biological family? Will Nina be the strength for her brother in his time of need? Will they ever find out what really happened to their mother?

In Stores!!!

Betrayal, lust, lies, murder, deception, sex and tainted love frame this story...
Julian Stevens lacks the ambition and freak ability that Miko looks for in a
man, but she married him despite his flaws to spite an ex-boyfriend. When
Miko least expects it, the old boyfriend shows up and ready to sweep her off
her feet again. Suddenly the grass grows greener on the other side, but Miko is
not an easily satisfied woman. She wants to have her cake and eat it too. While
Miko's doing her own thing, Julian is determined to become everything Miko
ever wanted in a man and more, but will he go to extreme lengths to prove he's
worthy of Miko's love? Julian Stevens soon finds out that he's capable of being
more than he could ever imagine as he embarks on a journey that will change
his life forever.

In Stores!!

The police in New York and other major cities around the country are increasingly victimizing black men. The violence has escalated to deadly force, most of the time without justification. In this controversial book, noted author Richard Jeanty, tackles the problem of police brutality and the unfair treatment of Black men at the hands of police in New York City and the rest of the country. The conflict between the Police and Black men will continue on a downward spiral until the mayors of every city hold accountable the members of their police force who use unnecessary deadly force against unarmed victims.

In Stores!!!

Just when Darren thinks his relationship with Tina is flourishing, there is yet another hurdle on the road hindering their bliss. Tina saw a therapist for months to deal with her sexual addiction, but now Darren is wondering if she was ever treated completely. Darren has not been taking care of home and Tina's frustrated and agrees to a break-up with Darren. Will Darren lose Tina for good? Will Tina ever realize that Darren is the best man for her?

In Stores!!

Ronald Murphy was a player all his life until he and his best friend, Myles, met the women of their dreams during a brief vacation in South Beach, Florida. Sexual Jeopardy is story of trust, betrayal, forgiveness, friendship, hope and HIV.

In Stores!!!

Tina develops an insatiable sexual appetite very early in life. She only loves her boyfriend, Darren, but he's too far away in college to satisfy her sexual needs.

Tina decides to get buck wild away in college

Will her sexual trysts jeopardize the lives of the men in her life?

In Stores!!!

Faith Jones, a woman in her mid-thirties, has given up on ever finding love again until she met her son's best friend, Darius. Faith Jones is walking a thin line of betrayal against her son for the love of Darius. Will Faith allow her emotions to outweigh her common sense?

In Stores!!!

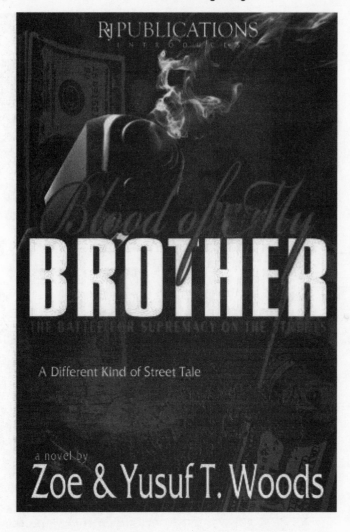

Roc was the man on the streets of Philadelphia, until his younger brother decided it was time to become his own man by wreaking havoc on Roc's crew without any regards for the blood relation they share. Drug, murder, mayhem and the pursuit of happiness can lead to deadly consequences. This story can only be told by a person who has lived it.

In Stores!!!

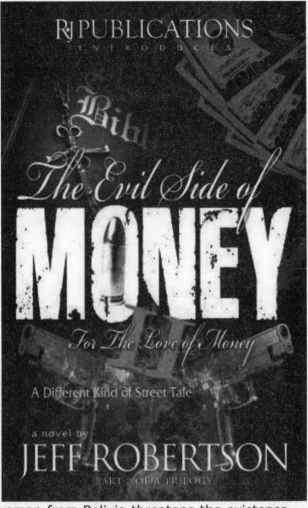

A beautigul woman from Bolivia threatens the existence of the drug empire that Nate and G have built. While Nate is head over heels for her, G can see right through her. As she brings on more conflict between the crew, G sets out to show Nate exactly who she is before she brings about their demise.

Coming in October 2008!!

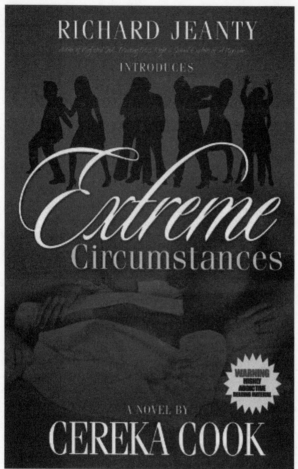

What happens when a devoted woman is betrayed? Come take a ride with Chanel as she takes her boyfriend, Donnell, to circumstances beyond belief after he betrays her trust with his endless infidelities. How long can Chanel's friend, Janai, use her looks to get what she wants from men before it catches up to her? Find out as Janai's gold-digging ways catch up with and she has to face the consequences of her extreme actions.

In Stores!!!

Violence, Intimidation and carnage are the order as Nathan and his
brother set out to build the most powerful drug empires in Chicago.
However, when God comes knocking, Nathan's conscience starts to
surface. Will his haunted criminal past get the best of him?
In Stores!!

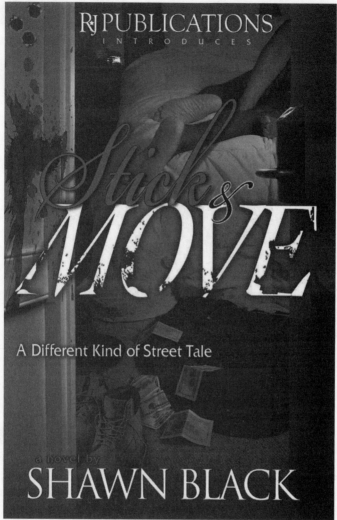

Yasmina witnessed the brutal murder of her parents at a young age at the hand of a drug dealer. This event stained her mind and upbringing as a result. Will Yamina's life come full circle with her past? Find out as Yasmina's crew, The Platinum Chicks, set out to make a name for themselves on the street.

In stores!!

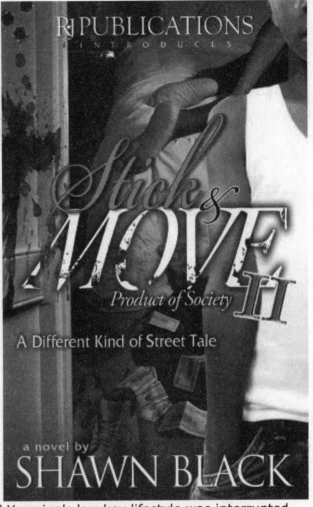

Scorcher and Yasmina's low key lifestyle was interrupted
when they were taken down by the Feds, but their
daughter, Serosa, was left to be raised by the foster
care system. Will Serosa become a product of her
environment or will she rise above it all? Her bloodline is
undeniable, but will she be able to control it?

Coming soon!!

Ashland's mother, Bianca, fights hard to suppress the truth from her daughter because she doesn't want her to marry Jordan, the grandson of an ex-lover she loathes. Ashland soon finds out how cruel and vengeful her mother can be, but what price will Bianca pay for redemption?

In stores!!

After Chasin' Satisfaction, Miko finds that satisfaction is not all
that it's cracked up to be. As a matter of fact, it left nothing
but death in its aftermath. Now living the glamorous life in
Miami while putting the finishing touches on his hybrid condo
hotel, Julian realizes with newfound success he's now become
the hunted. Julian's success is threatened as someone from his
past vows revenge on him.

Coming December 2008!!

An ex-drug dealer finds himself in a bind after he's caught by
the Feds. He has to decide which is more important, his family
or his loyalty to the game. As he fights hard to make a
decision, those who helped him to the top fear the worse from
him. Will he get the chance to tell the govt. whole story, or will
someone get to him before he becomes a snitch?

Coming October 2008!!

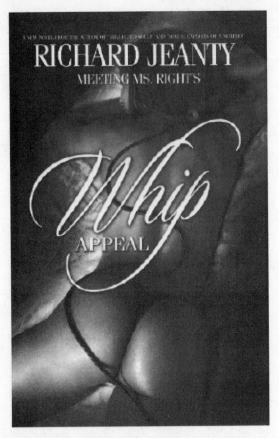

Malcolm is a wealthy virgin who decides to conceal his wealth
From the world until he meets the right woman. His wealthy best friend,
Dexter, hides his wealth from no one. Malcolm struggles to find love in
an environment where vanity and materialism are rampant, while Dexter
is getting more than enough of his share of women. Malcolm needs
develop self-esteem and confidence to meet the right woman and
Dexter's confidence is borderline arrogance.

Will bad boys like Dexter continue to take women for a ride?

Or will nice guys like Malcolm continue to finish last?

In Stores!!!

What happens when a woman's devotion to her fiancee is tested weeks before she gets married? What if her fiancee is just hiding behind the veil of ministry to deceive her? Find out as Sean Mitchell takes you on a journey you'll never forget into the lives of Angelica, Titus and Aurelius.

In Stores!!

PUBLICATIONS
BRINGING EXCITEMENT, FUN AND JOY TO READING

Use this coupon to order by mail

1. Neglected Souls, Richard Jeanty $14.95
2. Neglected No More, Richard Jeanty $14.95
3. Sexual Exploits of Nympho, Richard Jeanty $14.95
4. Meeting Ms. Right's Whip Appeal, Richard Jeanty $14.95
5. Me and Mrs. Jones, K.M Thompson ($14.95) Available
6. Chasin' Satisfaction, W.S Burkett ($14.95) Available
7. Extreme Circumstances, Cereka Cook ($14.95) Available
8. The Most Dangerous Gang In America, R. Jeanty $15.00
9. Sexual Exploits of a Nympho II, Richard Jeanty $15.00
10. Sexual Jeopardy, Richard Jeanty $14.95 Coming: 2/15/ 2008
11. Too Many Secrets, Too Many Lies, Sonya Sparks $15.00
12. Stick And Move, Shawn Black ($15.00) Coming 1/15/ 2008
13. Evil Side Of Money, Jeff Robertson $15.00
14. Cater To Her, W.S Burkett $15.00 Coming 3/30/ 2008
15. Blood of my Brother, Zoe & Ysuf Woods $15.00
16. Hoodfellas, Richard Jeanty $15.00 11/30/2008
17. The Bedroom Bandit, Richard Jeanty $15.00 January 2009

Name_____

Address_____

City_____State_____Zip Code_____

Please send the novels that I have circled above.

Shipping and Handling $1.99
Total Number of Books_____
Total Amount Due_____

This offer is subject to change without notice.

Send check or money order (no cash or CODs) to:
RJ Publications
290 Dune Street
Far Rockaway, NY 11691

For more information please call 718-471-2926, or visit
www.rjpublications.com

Please allow 2-3 weeks for delivery.

Use this coupon to order by mail

18. Neglected Souls, Richard Jeanty $14.95
19. Neglected No More, Richard Jeanty $14.95
20. Sexual Exploits of Nympho, Richard Jeanty $14.95
21. Meeting Ms. Right's Whip Appeal, Richard Jeanty $14.95
22. Me and Mrs. Jones, K.M Thompson ($14.95) Available
23. Chasin' Satisfaction, W.S Burkett ($14.95) Available
24. Extreme Circumstances, Cereka Cook ($14.95) Available
25. The Most Dangerous Gang In America, R. Jeanty $15.00
26. Sexual Exploits of a Nympho II, Richard Jeanty $15.00
27. Sexual Jeopardy, Richard Jeanty $14.95 Coming: 2/15/ 2008
28. Too Many Secrets, Too Many Lies, Sonya Sparks $15.00
29. Stick And Move, Shawn Black ($15.00) Coming 1/15/ 2008
30. Evil Side Of Money, Jeff Robertson $15.00
31. Cater To Her, W.S Burkett $15.00 Coming 3/30/ 2008
32. Blood of my Brother, Zoe & Ysuf Woods $15.00
33. Hoodfellas, Richard Jeanty $15.00 11/30/2008
34. The Bedroom Bandit, Richard Jeanty $15.00 January 2009

Name_____
Address_____
City_____State_____Zip Code_____

Please send the novels that I have circled above.

Shipping and Handling $1.99
Total Number of Books_____
Total Amount Due_____

This offer is subject to change without notice.

Send check or money order (no cash or CODs) to:
RJ Publications
290 Dune Street
Far Rockaway, NY 11691

For more information please call 718-471-2926, or visit
www.rjpublications.com

Please allow 2-3 weeks for delivery.

Hoodfellas   *Richard Jeanty*

PUBLICATIONS
BRINGING EXCITEMENT, FUN AND JOY TO READING

Use this coupon to order by mail

35. Neglected Souls, Richard Jeanty $14.95
36. Neglected No More, Richard Jeanty $14.95
37. Sexual Exploits of Nympho, Richard Jeanty $14.95
38. Meeting Ms. Right's Whip Appeal, Richard Jeanty $14.95
39. Me and Mrs. Jones, K.M Thompson ($14.95) Available
40. Chasin' Satisfaction, W.S Burkett ($14.95) Available
41. Extreme Circumstances, Cereka Cook ($14.95) Available
42. The Most Dangerous Gang In America, R. Jeanty $15.00
43. Sexual Exploits of a Nympho II, Richard Jeanty $15.00
44. Sexual Jeopardy, Richard Jeanty $14.95 Coming: 2/15/ 2008
45. Too Many Secrets, Too Many Lies, Sonya Sparks $15.00
46. Stick And Move, Shawn Black ($15.00) Coming 1/15/ 2008
47. Evil Side Of Money, Jeff Robertson $15.00
48. Cater To Her, W.S Burkett $15.00 Coming 3/30/ 2008
49. Blood of my Brother, Zoe & Ysuf Woods $15.00
50. Hoodfellas, Richard Jeanty $15.00 11/30/2008
51. The Bedroom Bandit, Richard Jeanty $15.00 January 2009

Name_____
Address_____
City_____State_____Zip Code_____

Please send the novels that I have circled above.

Shipping and Handling $1.99
Total Number of Books_____
Total Amount Due_____

This offer is subject to change without notice.

Send check or money order (no cash or CODs) to:
RJ Publications
290 Dune Street
Far Rockaway, NY 11691

For more information please call 718-471-2926, or visit www.rjpublications.com

Please allow 2-3 weeks for delivery.

PUBLICATIONS
BRINGING EXCITEMENT, FUN AND JOY TO READING

Use this coupon to order by mail

52. Neglected Souls, Richard Jeanty $14.95
53. Neglected No More, Richard Jeanty $14.95
54. Sexual Exploits of Nympho, Richard Jeanty $14.95
55. Meeting Ms. Right's Whip Appeal, Richard Jeanty $14.95
56. Me and Mrs. Jones, K.M Thompson ($14.95) Available
57. Chasin' Satisfaction, W.S Burkett ($14.95) Available
58. Extreme Circumstances, Cereka Cook ($14.95) Available
59. The Most Dangerous Gang In America, R. Jeanty $15.00
60. Sexual Exploits of a Nympho II, Richard Jeanty $15.00
61. Sexual Jeopardy, Richard Jeanty $14.95 Coming: 2/15/ 2008
62. Too Many Secrets, Too Many Lies, Sonya Sparks $15.00
63. Stick And Move, Shawn Black ($15.00) Coming 1/15/ 2008
64. Evil Side Of Money, Jeff Robertson $15.00
65. Cater To Her, W.S Burkett $15.00 Coming 3/30/ 2008
66. Blood of my Brother, Zoe & Ysuf Woods $15.00
67. Hoodfellas, Richard Jeanty $15.00 11/30/2008
68. The Bedroom Bandit, Richard Jeanty $15.00 January 2009

Name_____
Address_____
City_____State_____Zip Code_____

Please send the novels that I have circled above.

Shipping and Handling $1.99
Total Number of Books_____
Total Amount Due_____

This offer is subject to change without notice.

Send check or money order (no cash or CODs) to:
RJ Publications
290 Dune Street
Far Rockaway, NY 11691

For more information please call 718-471-2926, or visit
www.rjpublications.com

Please allow 2-3 weeks for delivery.